SUMMER ISLAND SISTERS

CIARA KNIGHT

Summer Island Sisters
Book I
Friendship Beach Series
Copyright ©2021 by Ciara Knight
All rights reserved.

Cover art by Yocla Cover Designs
Edited by Bev Katz Rosenbaum
Copy Edit by Jenny Rarden
Proofreading by Rachel

❀ Created with Vellum

READER LETTER

Dear Reader,

It has been so amazing visiting my hometown world and sharing it with all of you. While writing this story, I could feel the sun on my face, hear the seagulls squawking overhead, smell the damp asphalt as rain rolls in from the ocean. I hope I've managed to transport you from your hectic lives to this serene little corner of Florida, if only for a little while.

I've been receiving a lot of mail about how this series is such a joy since it focuses on mature women opposed to young adulthood. I hadn't realized that there was such a limited amount of stories about this stage in a woman's life, but I'm humbled and excited that I've provided something that was missing in your reading world.

I hope you enjoy this story as much as you enjoyed book I, Summer Island Book Club. If so, please take a second to leave a review on Amazon or another online retailer. This helps let me know you'd like this series to continue.

Happy reading!
Ciara

CHAPTER ONE

Home.

How could a single word carry so much meaning? To Trace Latimer, it meant childhood, friends, a feeling of being able to take on the world. And she had, even if she'd failed.

The broken gravel road pressed into the bottom of Trace's worn hiking sandals.

Julie "Jewels" Boone, Trace's best friend since forever, threw her arms around her. "Are you ready for an exciting spring break?"

Trace stumbled over loose pebbles, but Jewels caught her. The way she always had when they were kids. If only she would've been there to catch Trace before she'd fallen into the epic mess that kept her away so long. The mess that cost her saying goodbye to her father before he died.

"Kat and Wind should arrive tomorrow. I think Bri's more excited than I am to have some girl power in her life." Jewels flexed her bicep like the 1940s Rosie the Riveter poster.

Her childhood friends, Kat and Wind, plus Jewels's

daughter Bri would be a much-needed distraction from real life.

Waves crashed into the cement wall at the edge of the riverbank near the junction to the Atlantic Ocean as if in warning of an approaching storm. "How's Bri doing with her writing?"

Jewels shrugged. "Still working with an agent to edit the story. People want to read about midlife women and their friendships and romance. Who knew?"

Trace shoulder bumped her. "We're not in our dotage you know."

"Speak for yourself. You haven't hit the big 5-0 yet." A seagull applauded her dramatics with flapping wings and squawking. Obviously Jewels had taken a page out of their theatrical friend Wind's screenplay.

"Nope, still forty-nine. I'm the baby of our friend family. You, Cat, Wind, and then me. The youngest sister." Trace used to hate being referred to as the baby of the bunch, but now she embraced being the youngest. Funny how perception changed over the years.

The puffy clouds parted, allowing golden rays to shoot to the ground. Trace embraced the morning warmth on her face and her friend at her side. Did she deserve such comfort when she'd caused so much pain?

Jewels paused only a few steps from the sand, still in tune with Trace after all these years. "Hey."

Trace saw the tell-me-what's-wrong glance and shifted into avoidance. "I'm so happy I've had the chance to get to know Bri better. It's a shame all of us were apart for so long."

Jewels looked down her perfect nose at Trace, waiting for more.

Trace longed to fall on her knees and confess to her best friend the sins of her past. About her assistant Matt and how her distraction with oil tycoon Robert Remming had cost Matt his life. Her stomach dipped and dove into the queasy pit of regrets.

Thankfully, Jewels didn't press the subject. At the edge of the broken road, they slipped off their sandals and stepped onto the beach. The sand between Trace's toes soothed and welcomed her to the small beach at the edge of Banana River. A stark contrast from the hard and dangerous oil rig she'd left behind weeks ago.

Images of corporate corruption and confrontation and cold hard truths flashed. The hair on Trace's neck prickled like a porcupine fish.

"But we're together now. I'm so excited to have Bri and you home with me." Jewels slid her arm into Trace's.

Trace didn't like too much physical contact. It made her uneasy. Perhaps it was from growing up with no mother or sisters.

"You don't mind that she gave up her fancy career to move back to Summer Island?" Trace treaded more carefully in conversation than through the sand.

Jewels sighed, the way only a mother who loved her daughter could sigh. "Honestly, I don't care. I love having her here. I tried to push her out of the nest because I was trying to live vicariously through her. In the end, I realized my small-town life wasn't a letdown compared to the grand living you and Kat and Wind have experienced, but a gift."

"You have no idea." Trace bit her bottom lip, but it was too late. The words had already spilled out into the world. She held her breath, waiting for Jewels's onslaught of questions, but to her relief, Jewels was lost in her own thoughts.

"This change in career makes her happy, so I'm glad she gave up her big-time job for a simpler life with me."

"Family's important." Trace took in a breath of salty air with a hint of brackish odor from the nearby canals. The smells coated her senses and fueled her guilt. He was gone.

"I'm sorry your father passed away," Jewels whispered, as if saying it too loud made it hurt worse.

Trace shrugged. "I'm sorry your husband passed." She winked at Jewels. "Glad you found a new tall, not-so-dark, and sexy sailor."

Jewels beamed with that new-love look. "I'm glad we're both moving on." She slowed her pace. "Are you sure you're ready to face your childhood home? You've been through a lot lately, and I'm afraid you'll be disappointed when you see how run down it is."

What did she mean *a lot lately*? She couldn't know what happened. "It's only been a year since I was here last. I'm ready." Wanting to change the subject to avoid the gnawing pain that she hadn't been here for her father when he had died, she quickened her steps. "How's Friendship Beach?"

"Nice avoidance." Jewels stopped dead a few feet from the backyard of her new boyfriend's place. "I know Trace Latimer doesn't discuss emotions and feelings, but I want you to know that I'm here if you need me."

Trace stiffened. No way she'd open that ocean-filled Pandora's box of ragged and jagged emotions. "So Bri and you haven't kept up the beach like you promised?"

"No, we have." She shook her head. "Trace…"

"I heard you, okay?" Trace snugged her arm tighter and hip bumped her. "Not now."

Even if she wanted to, she couldn't talk now. Not when gag orders and secrets sealed her mouth. Not when she'd been the cause of so much pain. Not when she was looking for respite in her life.

Jewels took the hip hint and sauntered toward her boyfriend's backyard. "Trevor won't step foot on Friendship Beach without express permission from you, Wind, and Kat. He says he won't mess with the Summer Island Book Club if he wants to live."

Trace paused at the edge of the docks that served as Trevor's new chartering business and looked to the other side of the channel. She spotted the little peninsula with jagged rocks that protected the lagoon. The overhanging mangroves hid the entrance to the tiny canal and their personal, private, protected hideout since childhood.

Relieved that they'd restored the beach area a few months ago, she felt a pin-prick of success, but it was hidden beneath the open wound of losing the big battle in Brazil. She shook off the memory before it took hold and stowed her grief. Feelings were meant to be experienced, not talked about. "What do you think we'll do this week besides our book club?"

"Wind has all sorts of nonsense planned with theatrical games and girl time. I think she needs something to focus on since her Broadway show was cut. She's searching for a new choreography job."

"I'm not putting on a costume and performing for the town." Trace snickered, but it was more of an exhausted chortle than humor. She was midlife, yet fatigue made her feel end-of-life.

"You know it's your turn to pick the book, right?" Jewels said in an I've-got-a-secret tone.

"No, seriously? I'm sure Wind will take this year."

"Nope. All you." Jewels tugged her toward the path that led to Trace's childhood home.

Her chest tightened.

A pelican swooped in and grabbed a fish. Trace watched the natural order of things and shook off the feeling she'd been a minnow in shark-infested waters when she'd taken on the oil giants. She'd been so sure, so strong, so stupid.

Jewels released her but didn't stop the analytical gaze on her face. "Listen, you can stay with me for as long as you like."

Then she shouldered Trace. "Come on. You'll bounce back. Trace Latimer's a fighter for sea otters and whale sharks and all things living. Except for herself."

"What's that supposed to mean?" Trace stopped at the edge of the yard not far from her path, the one from her childhood. She'd loved every minute of her tomboy, no shoes or rules kind of upbringing.

Jewels looked to the puffy white clouds that promised a gorgeous day. "Listen, you take on fights for everyone else, but when will you fight for your own happiness?"

"Just because you're in love doesn't mean I have to be, too." Trace stepped onto the cracked asphalt patch filled with erupting roots at the edge of the broken-down hotel at which she'd worked as a maid while in high school. Its crooked shutters and dirty windows made it look haunted with past memories. Memories that would be destroyed by the renovating and modernizing of the hotel by Trevor's best friend, Dustin Hawk. The hunk-of-a-mess Trace wanted to stay away from. "You're the settle down type. I'm the keep moving type."

"That's it, you keep moving. Why don't you ever stop?"

Trace halted her steps at the end of the white sand beach that appeared to be cleaned up, despite the lack of use from hotel guests. "I've stopped now. There's a fight here on Summer Island. I'm home, and I'm going to fix up my old

6

house and live there while I fight Dustin on turning the old hotel into some trendy, touristy condos that look out of place in Summer Island."

"Oh, no, what have you done?"

Trace lifted her chin. "I filed a stop order due to historical reasons."

"You didn't." Jewels sighed. "I love having you back here, but do you have to stir up trouble with my boyfriend's best friend?"

A twinge of guilt pinched her chest, but she couldn't give in to the businessman-without-a-heart type again. "Sorry about that. I'm not trying to stop him, just keep him from ruining our town. I'm staying for a while to make sure he doesn't do anything to hurt Summer Island. Trust me, I know the big business types."

"Fine, but you're staying with me. You don't need to live in your childhood home."

"The house is on the most beautiful spot on the island, so I'll fix it up and enjoy the view. I'll even tear down the old shack in the woods we used to play in as kids. That will give me a clear line of sight to keep an eye on Dustin Hawk. Once I figure out where to go next, and the hotel's finished, I'll use this place as a vacation escape to come home for book club and my friendsters."

"Friendsters?" Jewels raised a that's-a-new-one-to-me brow.

"Haven't you read your own daughter's book? That's what she calls us. The friends that are more like sisters —friendsters."

"It must have been added to one of her revisions, because that wasn't in the original I read."

Trace pushed back branches of overgrown shrubs, shuffled

through weeds, and hopped over downed tree branches to find the overgrown path to her property. "Aren't you the one who pressured me the last few months to come home and take up my fight here?"

"Yes, but not this way. Not when you're upset over what happened. Not when you insist on moving into a place that doesn't have air conditioning. You need to stay with me."

The uneasy sound of her voice made Trace decide she needed to shut down everyone tip-toeing around her for the next week, worried about her facing the death of her father and why she'd left her work behind.

Trace hot-footed it over prickly plants and old haunts with Jewels at her heels until she reached the clearing to find her home. She didn't stop at the overgrown weeds covering the beauty of the land. She didn't stop at the sight of the vegetation eating away at the structure. She didn't stop at the busted window, shattered beyond repair.

She halted at the sign written in bold red letters nailed to the front door.

9:00 AM April 4th Demolition.

CHAPTER TWO

THE CHIPMUNK-SIZED old man wearing a beanie hat hunched over the counter and eyed Dustin Hawk with the gaze of a lion ready to attack. "Work stop order's official." He slammed his liver-spotted hand against the counter. His splayed fingers covered the stop order, and his shoulders squared like a general dressing down his men.

Trevor Ashford, Dustin's oldest and dearest friend, tugged him away from the Summer Island Courthouse front counter. "We better go before you do something stupid."

Dustin lowered his voice to under eighty-year-old volume. "Don't worry. I know how to deal with men like him." He pulled a hundred from his pocket, slapped it on the counter, and slid it to the man. "I realize it's official, but you look like the person who's in charge around here."

The man picked up the hundred with shaking hands, looked at it, opened the folded bill, analyzed it some more, shrugged, and then shoved it into his pocket. "Don't know why you gave me this, but Papa needs a new pair of slippers."

He stuck his leg around the tall reception desk and shook his foot, making the bunny ears come to life.

"It's to help with the…um…"

Trevor clapped him on the shoulder. "Don't go there."

"It's how business is done, or have you forgotten?" Dustin lifted a brow.

Trevor held up his hands and backed away with a grin and a snicker. "You always did have to learn things the hard way."

"Sir."

"Name's Mr. Mannie. Says so right here." He pointed to an old wooden nameplate that looked like it was left over from the Dark Ages. Tape covered the last name, all except a W.

"Right. Mr. Mannie. That hundred is for an expedited processing fee so that the stop order can be lifted and I can resume work on the hotel. The hotel that will bring a boost to the Summer Island economy."

"Never heard of no expedited processing fee. We don't have those here." He adjusted his hat as if the bill was blocking his view.

Dustin guessed the Coke-bottle thick glasses on the counter were probably his, and the man couldn't even see what he'd slid into his pocket. "Right, but that was a hundred dollars."

"Yeah, and?"

"And it should help move things forward so that I can get my hotel up and running."

Mr. Mannie shuffled over to the calendar. "Don't know how that could be. Town meetin's on the sixth. Can't expedite nothin' till then."

Obviously the man wasn't understanding Dustin's meaning. "Right, but that hundred dollars I gave you could help *you* expedite the process so that I can get back to work."

Trevor tugged at Dustin's sleeve.

Mr. Mannie jutted out his lower lip, making his face look like a gnome. "Can't do no such thing."

"But you can. You work here." Dustin nudged him toward the truth. "I paid you so that you could get the job done now."

"I can't accept direct payments. Only gifts."

"Then we'll call it a gift."

He held up one knobby finger and shuffled away.

Dustin turned to Trevor. "See, I told you it'd work."

Mr. Mannie disappeared through the back door.

"I blame you. If you hadn't convinced me to come here and help you with your business, I wouldn't be in this situation," Dustin huffed.

"If you hadn't come here, you wouldn't have gotten away from the dreary northwest, the big city politics, and closer to one Trace Latimer."

"Who?" Dustin attempted to hide his Summer Island crush, but based on Trevor's crossed arms, legs, and attitude, he wasn't successful. "You mean Rhonda. Yep, she's been helping me with this small-town business stuff, unlike my best friend."

"I'm here watching you make a fool out of yourself, aren't I? Besides, I warned you about Rhonda and her reputation."

Dustin laughed. "I'm not dating her. She's a nice, simple woman trying to do good things for her community."

Trevor smacked his forehead as if ending a mosquito assault on his skin. "You can't be that naive. That woman doesn't care about her community. She only cares about sticking it to Jewels and her friends. It's some sort of child-hood feud that never ended. You better be careful."

"You might want to talk to your girlfriend about letting old grudges go. Rhonda's only wanted to be friends with

11

them." Dustin was thankful when the back door opened again.

"Got someone here to help." Mr. Mannie shuffled out of the back door, pink bunny ears bouncing, followed by a man dressed in a police uniform. "That's the man. He's offering bribes."

Dustin shot his palms out as if to block the officer's advance. "Whooa, wait a second. Not a bribe. A gift."

Trevor tugged at the back of his dress shirt, popping a button. "Let's go before you make things worse for yourself."

The officer, adjusting his oversized belt of weapons, stood with feet hip-width apart. "Let me ask you. Did you give Mr. Mannie a hundred dollars for new slippers or for him to illegally lift the stop work order on your hotel?"

Dustin looked to Trevor, who back stepped to the exit sign, looked to Mr. Mannie, who had a you-think-you're-so-smart toothless grin, and then looked to the officer, who reached for his cuffs. "Gift. New slippers. See you at the town meeting."

Trevor yanked Dustin out the door. He didn't resist this time. Before they reached the end of the sidewalk, he turned to face the building. "You've pulled me out of a flaming bureaucratic mess and thrown me into a bonfire crazy town."

"I tried to warn you that the scummy tactics you're used to incorporating into your business plan will only damage your reputation in Summer Island." Trevor pointed up the street to two women power walking toward them. "Looks like Jewels and Trace are done at her dad's place already."

Dustin's pulse skipped and face planted at the feet of one blonde-haired, blue-eyed, so-wrong-for-him Trace Latimer.

"You might want to wipe the drool off your chin." Trevor

laughed like a seal in heat and abandoned Dustin's side once again for something better.

Jewels Boone.

Watching Trevor scoop Jewels into his arms, spinning her around, made Dustin's sushi lunch swim. Trace didn't seem to notice since she was making a beeline to the building. He cleared his throat. "Hi, Trace. I heard you were going to be back in town this week. What's been going on?"

Pathetic.

Why did this woman always twist him up? He never had problems talking to women. Heck, he never had to open his mouth since women tended to throw themselves at him. Maybe that's why he found Trace so intriguing. He didn't understand her. The woman attacked her philanthropic pursuits with passion and prickles.

Trevor had told him stories he'd heard from Jewels about how Trace had camped out for weeks in front of a courthouse to stop some big business from developing a condo due to impact on ecosystems, spent a year in frigid Antarctica to protect penguins, and months fighting some oil tycoon off the coast of some third world country to stop drilling. If only she could have passion for humans. She certainly had none for him, and he wanted to know why.

Trace narrowed her gaze. "What are you doing here? I thought you'd go chasing some woman back to city life by now," Trace said in a glacier tone.

"Is that what you think of me? A womanizer?" If he were honest with himself, he knew she wasn't far from the truth. He had been voted Most Eligible Playboy in the Northwest two years in a row. But he'd come here to change that. To follow his best friend down the path of sunshine and happiness and a real future with the right woman. But he'd stumbled into the wrong, so wrong for him, abrasive, hauntingly beautiful Trace. And like gum to a shoe, he'd been stuck on pause and rewind. This needed to stop.

She laughed. "I know your type. You use your charms and good looks to sway a girl's opinion. Don't worry. I won't fall for your manipulations. I'm immune."

The woman was too hostile and too rude. "I knew you were attracted to me." Why was she so hostile? "Sorry you're scared of your feelings."

"Scared? No, hon. I just don't want you ripping apart a Summer Island historical site. Not going to happen. I'm not going to be manipulated into backing down. I'll make sure you don't destroy the charm of the Summer Island Hotel."

"You're the reason I can't fix the hotel." Despite his attraction, and a hint of respect for her bold move, he didn't lose. Especially to some tree hugger who knew nothing about real business. "I heard you were difficult and stubborn. Maybe Rhonda's right and you're insecure."

Her face turned northerner-lobster-sunburn color. "Go back to the big city and take over heartless companies. You're out of your league here. I'll best you every time." She wrenched open the Summer Island Courthouse door. "Word of advice. Don't listen to anything that woman says. She only wants to stir up trouble."

"Best me? You obviously don't know who I am." That came out more arrogant than he'd meant, but it was the truth. He was a powerful businessman who knew his way around the conference table.

"I'll win. These are my people."

Before he could respond, she bolted inside the courthouse,

obviously plotting her next sinister move to thwart his business. He wouldn't allow it. She wanted to play dirty? He'd dig himself into the mud pit of small-town politics.

CHAPTER THREE

THIS WAS TRACE'S HOMETOWN, not Dustin Hawk's. She would win the fight to preserve the historical charm of the hotel if it meant she had to be the zoning police. That was tomorrow's problem. Today, she needed to make up for past sins and stop the demolition of her father's home. "Hey Mr. Mannie, what's been cooking in that smoker of yours?"

Mr. Mannie slid his glasses up his nose that had grown as fast as his body had shrunk in the last few years. "Don't go tricking me into spillin' no info. Not gonna work."

"What?" She hopped up on the table against the wall and forced a beachy calm despite the acidic waves in her gut. "I'm only here to spend some time with my favorite Summer Island gentleman. You're an extinct breed."

His shoulders lowered below his dangling earlobes. How a man with everything sagging and aging and sun-damaged still looked handsome, she would wonder the rest of her days. Had to be his eyes, those silver ones Jewels's neighbor and Summer Island lifer, Mrs. Watermore, called Sinatra blue. "I know why you're here. Nothin' I can do 'bout no order to tear your pop's place down. Don't mean I agree with it, though."

"Who does? That's what I'm confused about." Trace swung her legs and tilted her head in a schoolgirl-on-the-playground way. "My town would never demolish the home of a great man. A man who looked out for the residents for decades. A man who organized and ran sandbagging before hurricanes. A man who fought the state politicians when they wanted to seize sections of our land. A man who pulled you out of a mangled car and breathed life back into your lungs. No, the town would never destroy the legacy of that man."

Mr. Mannie pounded his fist against the front desk. "Now why'd ya go and make me feel like that for?" He shuffled over to a computer left over from the brick and mortar store days, hunt-and-pecked for almost two minutes. "Can't tell you no secret town business. I'd be fired. Can't lose this job. It's all I's got. Except keeping watch on my town."

Mr. Mannie was the unofficial neighborhood watch president of all things of interest. And he did that well. Living on the stretch of beach from Sunset to her father's place, he watched all the happenings on that side of town, while the owner of Summer Sweets, Mrs. Graysen, handled the other side. No one could get away with anything in Summer Island without it ending up on the Salty Breeze Gossip Line in minutes. The SBGL worked faster than 10G.

"I don't want anyone to lose their job, so I won't say anything to anyone. It's just that I can't let my father down. Not again." She bowed her head in I-abandoned-my-only-family-to-protect-sea-creatures shame.

"Prodigal tomboy returns." He took off his glasses, tossed them onto the desk, and looked at her with narrowed eyes.

"That's me, returned to set things right. Not only for me,

but for the town. We need to stick together to preserve our history."

"Don't disagree." He patted his front pocket and pulled out his glasses case, looked inside, and then slid it back into his pocket. "Dagnabbit. I lost my glasses again." He turned in all directions and then halted and blinked at her. With his gaze trained on her, he nudged the screen around toward her. "Guess I left 'em in the back. Return in two shakes of a shark's tail. Don't go doing anything wrong out here while I'm gone." He pointed a knobby finger at the screen and then shuffled out of the room.

Trace bolted from the table, hurtled a small stool, and eyed the screen. "Rhonda Shaker reported rat infestation. I knew it." She fisted her hands. At the bottom of the screen, she found the name of the demolition company, and next to it was a note.

Demolition handled by Dustin Hawk.

Trace's blood boiled like a volcano on doomsday. She'd take that Dustin Hawk and force him from Summer Island before she'd let him touch her father's house.

The front door opened with a smiling Jewels, obviously done consorting with her enemy's best friend. "Oh, no. What happened, and who are you about to turn into chum?"

Trace marched past her and headed up the street.

Jewels reached her side, panting. "Wait. Tell me before I have to bail you out of jail again."

She halted at the ugly reminder. "That was once, and I didn't mean for you to get thrown in with me. All over a stupid prank to bring awareness to the principal's desire to murder animals."

"You put red paint all over her mink coat."

"It's not like she needed it. Didn't the woman understand

18

you don't need heavy coats in Florida? Besides, I did her a favor. It looked ridiculous. Almost as ridiculous as Mr. Mannie's leopard print speedo." Trace shivered at the vision.

She stepped to the side, but Jewels blocked her advance. "Move, or you'll end up collateral damage. Rhonda has gone too far this time, and Dustin is a puppet in her game. Either willing or unwilling, he means to tear down my father's house."

She couldn't let that happen. She couldn't let someone else down. Not now, not ever again.

"If that's the case, I'll help. I have connections, you know." She winked, as if Trace hadn't heard all about her spending every millisecond of every day with Trevor since they'd met. "We have until tomorrow morning before they'll even attempt to tear down the house. Let me try to resolve this peacefully before you put Rhonda at the bottom of the ocean."

"You make that sound like a bad thing."

Jewels wrapped her arm around Trace in a straight-jacket grip. "Come on. I'll call Rhonda and try to reason with her. Better yet, I'll get Bri to do it. She's great at negotiating. If that doesn't work, I'll go talk to Trevor to get Dustin to stand down. I can't believe that Trevor knew anything about this. Maybe Dustin doesn't know it's your father's house. He only arrived a few weeks ago."

Trace knew that yelling at Rhonda and empty threats weren't going to change anything. And at that moment, she wasn't sure she wouldn't resort to more drastic measures, so she walked side by side with her best friend in hopes that Jewels would save the day once again. The way she'd saved Trace from jail after she'd let all the air out of the bus tires to stop the emissions from killing all the plant and animal and human lives on the planet. Trace had been hotheaded in her youth but thought she'd grown into a real civilized pro-rights fighter. That's what Robert had told her, that she was the first activist he'd ever met who made him want to work harder to preserve the environment.

How had she been so stupid?

Jewels opened the front door of the house.

Their mischievous pet ferret, Houdini, shot through the dog door and up onto his platform. He never liked missing any drama.

Bri hopped up from the kitchen table and circled Trace, lifting one arm and then the other as if giving her some skin cancer exam. "I don't see any blood."

As if the lack of bloodshed was disappointing to Houdini, he raced down the gangway and disappeared into her room. The mischievous rodent unnerved Trace. Houdini liked to dig into stuff and she had a letter she'd written to Matt's family she didn't want discovered.

"I'll go check on Houdini. Be right back." She slipped into the guest room and found him eyeing her hiding spot taped to the bottom of the dresser. "Don't even think about it." She ripped it free and slid it into the underwear drawer. She knew she should rip it to shreds, but she couldn't. Despite the gag order, she longed to tell Matt's family the truth about what really happened to their son. "Be good."

Houdini settled on the bed, so Trace returned to the living room "Did you get her to call yet?"

"Call who?" Bri asked.

"Would you call Rhonda and speak with her? I'm thinking she'll be less threatened by you than one of us," Jewels asked in her sweetest I-know-you'll-do-this-for-me tone.

Bri shrugged. "What for?"

"She's trying to tear down my home so she can have an

ocean view. The woman's been trying since she bought her house fifteen years ago. She's tried a lot of stunts to get the property, but this is the closest she's ever gotten to destroying my home."

Home. That word sent a zap down her spine. Matt would never make it home again.

"Gotcha. Okay, I'll call her. What can I say to convince her to change her mind?"

"I won't kill her," Trace said.

"Right. How about I speak with her about a compromise? That usually helps in business, right?"

"That's a great idea," Jewels said.

"Sure, I'll compromise. I won't kill her if she doesn't tear down my place."

"I had something more constructive in mind." Bri tapped her lips with her pencil. The girl still wrote with paper and pen instead of a computer. Trace tried not to mention how many trees were slaughtered for one manuscript. "If she wants a view, why don't we agree that she can level the trees on the side of your home and the old clubhouse shack so she can see the ocean?"

"What? No. Then I have to look at the hotel out my side window."

"A tiny window in the bathroom you have to stand on your toes to see out of? In a house you haven't been in for three years?"

Ouch. That stung. Trace bit her bottom lip, not wanting to offer any compromise, but knew she had to give something. "Old shack is fine, though. It wasn't even good when we were kids."

Bri nodded. "It's a start."

"Make the call." Trace pointed to the cell phone on the

table. "If she doesn't agree, you two stay at the house while I pay her a friendly visit so you're not accomplices."

Bri took her cell phone and went outside. Probably a wise move, considering Trace wouldn't be able to hold her tongue. She paced the kitchen floor with Jewels watching her every move.

"You think she'll go for it?" Trace asked, her gut twisting with indecision. Part of her wanted Rhonda to refuse so she'd have an excuse to fight, but the other part only wanted to make things right for her father. She owed him this much.

Jewels cleared her throat. "Hon, tell me what's got you all torn up. I know you."

Trace rubbed the sting in her sternum. "It's my father's place."

"It's more, and we both know it." Jewels patted the seat by her side, but Trace couldn't stop moving because each time she slowed down, the memories caught up.

How could she tell her best friend she'd signed a gag order to avoid Robert Remming's company filing a report implicating her in the death of Matt to the Brazilian authorities? It didn't matter that she didn't know what he'd planned. Ultimately, it was her fault. If she hadn't told Matt all her war stories, he wouldn't have been inspired to do something so stupid.

Trace ignored her invitation and grabbed a glass from the cabinet and filled it with water. "Don't you think I feel guilty about not being here when my father needed me most?"

"He told me he sent you letters, but you said you didn't get them."

"I didn't," she snapped. The thread keeping her temper tied down broke.

"Then how is it your fault you weren't here? God rest his

soul, it was your father's fault. He chose not to send for you and made me vow to let him be the one to tell you. And then it was too late. If it's anyone's fault, it's mine."

"No." Trace set the glass down, unable to swallow the liquid or fear. "It's not. I should've been here. I saw him last year and knew he wasn't well. He hid it, but not well enough." She gripped the counter. "Why didn't he want me here?"

"I don't know, hon, but I guess he never wanted to cage the bird. That's what he'd said anyway. You know he was so proud of you. I think you lived the life he always wanted."

Dryness choked Trace into silence. She took a swig of water, but it didn't cool her throat or her pain.

"I spoke to Rhonda." Bri returned with a guilty, downcast gaze.

Welcoming the interruption, Trace turned on her heels and shut the grief back into its cage. "What?" she asked.

Bri stood on the other side of the table, as if scared to share the news. "She said that wouldn't work."

"What?" Trace ground out like rubble into dust. She took a breath, cooling her temper. "Is that all she said?"

Bri looked to Jewels, obviously for motherly advice.

"Go ahead and say exactly what Rhonda told you."

"She said, 'Now that I have her by her high-and-mighty fins, she's going to make a deal. Not a snowball's chance in Summer Island would I agree to a compromise when I can watch her childhood home being turned to kindling.'"

Trace lunged for the door. "That vicious…"

"Wait." Jewels blocked her exit. "We have another move here. Trevor. Don't give up hope yet."

"Hope? No. I hope he can't help so I can put an end to this thirty-year feud the way I wanted to in high school."

CHAPTER FOUR

DUSTIN WASN'T GOING to sit around and wait any longer. He washed his lunch dish and stuck it in the rack. The taste of day-old bread and failure stuck around. "Rhonda's right. Trace only cares about sticking it to people."

They stood in the main room of Trevor's too-small-for-them-both home, but until Dustin renovated one of the hotel rooms, he'd have to stay put. "I think you're mad because you thought you'd waltz into Summer Island and have it easy compared to the bureaucratic mess you had in Seattle. Every city has its procedures."

"I have work to do," he grumbled.

"You're upset because Trace isn't interested in your game."

"Game? What game? I'm not playing around here. She's the one acting all self-important and dictating my life."

Trevor put on his readers and flopped onto the couch. "You're going to make things worse. Wait for the town meeting and present your case." He picked up his phone, probably for some sappy text from Jewels.

Dustin opened the glass sliding door to exit the suffocating house and conversation. "Last time I listened to you, I ended up living in Summer Island. I think I'll follow my own instincts. I'll get this hotel up and running, and then I'm going to find my next project far from here." He didn't really mean what he said. He liked Summer Island, despite the icy welcome he'd received from locals. The weather was much better than the dreary Pacific Northwest, and despite his puppy-love, stomach-churning ways, Dustin enjoyed hanging out with Trevor. It was like their college days.

At the edge of the back deck, he stopped and eyed the ocean, not sure if he was more averse to sharks or the people in this town. Footsteps followed. Undoubtedly Trevor would try to thwart his plans.

"Offer still stands to get you over your fear of the water." Trevor waltzed by him with an air that he owned the world. A stark change from a few months ago when he had faced the possibility of being a father with his so-wrong-for-him-ex-wife and losing the woman he obviously loved more than breathing.

"Don't need to get in the water to work on the hotel." Dustin kept in step with Trevor down the street. "I can't believe you like this town so much. All the times you raved about the people and the life here was a lie, wasn't it?" He wanted to believe the bait Trevor used to reel him into this place, but he hadn't witnessed this miraculous welcome.

Trevor buckled his tool belt around his waist as if he'd really get the work on the dock done today. Usually Dustin would help with Trevor's work, but not that close to the water. "No, you just need to stop fighting and start accepting this way of life. Once I did that, I found real happiness—not the kind you buy, the kind you earn."

"I'll accept this place when they do things my way." Dustin

eyed the hotel and all the tractors sitting abandoned on his property. "Tell me how it's fair to fine a business for equipment being left on its own land when they put a stop order on construction for historical violations."

"Because you didn't ask the council's permission to change the hotel, only to fix it."

"It needs an update if it's going to attract tourists." Dustin rubbed his throbbing temples.

"That's your first mistake. I told you they don't like tourists around here."

"Who doesn't want business? These people are crazy."

"Maybe, but I've already had weekly bookings, and with the tax breaks and low cost of living, I'm doing well. You can have that too—an easier life."

Dustin huffed. "Easier? Trace thwarts me at every turn. The fine was her doing."

"No, I doubt that." Trevor waved him off and stepped onto the dock, halting Dustin's steps.

"You're blind by your infatuation with Jewels, and you're worried about stirring up trouble with her and her friends. I'm not scared of them, though."

"You should be."

"I'll wait until the meeting to do any work on the hotel. Not because I'm scared of Trace and her little friend group but because I need to be smarter about this. I need more people on my side. In the meantime, I'll go ahead and demolish that monstrosity of a shack in the woods by the hotel. *That* I have permission to do."

"Yes, but you don't own that land, so you can't turn it into a day spa. The county only agreed to demolish the shack because they believed it was too broken to be fixed and useless to anyone. Some abandoned workshop in the woods. That's what you told me, right?"

"Rhonda says they'll sell me the land once I show that I'm willing to work with the townspeople. I can take down those few trees and add on to the hotel."

"Is it really worth it for a little strip of woods? Seriously? You still don't get it. Your money isn't going to make things happen here. Have you not been paying attention? And for a man voted Most Eligible Playboy of the Northwest, you sure don't have a clue about women. I'm telling you, Rhonda's using you. I don't know what she's planning, but she's going to get you to do the dirty work." Trevor gripped his head as if to keep it attached to his shoulders. "If you follow what she's telling you, this is going to end in disaster. Did you forget how I had to win over the town before I could even move forward with my boat charter business?"

Dustin tsked. "I thought that was just Jewels playing games to get your attention."

Trevor tossed his hand as if throwing a ball to him. "I give up."

"You can't give up. You're the reason I'm here."

"No. You didn't come here for me. You came here to find your own happiness with Trace. And she doesn't want you and your ego."

"Harsh." Dustin kicked the spear-sized splinter sticking up at the edge of the dock. "I'm not like you. Not going to lose myself to win some woman over." Dustin didn't like the way his chest fluttered each time Trace came near him. It only ever lasted a few seconds, though, before she said something to make him mad.

Trevor studied the lines on his sailboat bopping back and forth from a powerboat wake. "You really don't have a clue. I'll bet you two days of cooking duties that Trace will have you wrapped around her will by the end of the week."

"I'll take that bet. But how are you going to prove something like that?"

Trevor's mouth curled into a joker grin. "Because she'll get you to do something you don't want to do."

"Never." Dustin was sure of that.

"Ha. I'll even take it a step further. She'll get you to do something none of the rest of us can convince you to try."

"What's that?"

"Swim in the ocean."

Dustin shot his hand out, ready to shake on that sucker bet, but remained firmly planted on the safe cement wall. The gateway between soft grass and spiky dock. "I'll take that and raise you a week of dishes and laundry."

Trevor raced to him with outstretched hand. "And mowing the lawn shirtless wearing the pink apron we found when you moved in."

They shook, and Dustin knew he'd be relaxing for a month watching his friend do the chores, because no one would ever get him to swim in open water, where sharks and gators and all sorts of creatures lived. As far as he was concerned, that was their home and he didn't have any right to invade it. Never, ever going to happen. That was one thing he could be more certain of than his ability to run a company.

"I bet you're thinking there's no way I'll win, but I assure you that if Trace asks you for anything, you'll give it to her."

"That woman is nothing but rude. Not going to happen."

"It is. You're only upset because you finally met a woman who doesn't bow to your every whim." Trevor adjusted his work belt. "As a matter of fact, you're the girl this time. You'll do anything she asks."

He didn't bother to say another word at his friend's preposterous statement. "I'm going to make some calls. There are deals to be made in this town, and I'm going to make them. I'll beat Trace at her own game." That woman couldn't get him to skip rocks across the water, let alone swim. Sure she was pretty, but she was a pain, too. The last thing he needed in his life was a woman like Trace, and he'd make sure that never happened.

CHAPTER FIVE

TRACE TUGGED the metal chain out of the old barrel and dropped it into a wheelbarrow at the side of Jewels's storage shack turned art studio in her backyard.

Clank. Clink. Clunk.

The metal on metal made an awful racket, but she didn't stop, not until the entire hundred feet or so was loaded into the wheelbarrow.

Jewels poked her head out of the house, wiping her hands on a dishtowel. "What're you doing?"

"Stopping the demolition of my house. It's happening at nine this morning, so I need to get over there." She'd spent all night thinking of ways to follow Jewels's advice and talk her way through it, but people didn't listen. Dustin didn't listen.

"I told you I spoke to Trevor. He assured me he'll speak with Dustin. He had no idea that it was your house they were trying to tear down. He thought it was the old shack in the woods between the hotel and your property. That's what Rhonda had told them anyway. He's sure Dustin didn't know it was your home."

"Don't trust Dustin Hawk and his big-headed business."

Jewels removed her apron and crumbled it into a wad. "Wait for me. You're going to do something stupid and dangerous." Jewels disappeared into the house, but Trace eyed her watch and decided she didn't have time to waste. With all her strength, she lifted the handles and pushed the wheelbarrow down the cobblestone walk. The sand would be too difficult to push through, so she hung a left and headed for Main Street.

By the time she reached the corner, her arms were shaking from the strain and her calves were burning.

Honk. Honk.

Jewels pulled up by her side in her little Toyota. "You can't get that all the way to your dad's place." She flung the driver's side door open, went to the back, and popped the trunk. "We'll put it in my car and drive it over."

"No time." Trace lifted the wheelbarrow a few inches but didn't take another step, knowing Jewels was right. Even if she could make it, she wouldn't arrive in time.

"We'll leave the wheelbarrow here, and I'll drive through the pass and straight to the back door of the house." Jewels nudged Trace out of the way and wheeled the chain to the back of her car.

Trace helped her load the thick, rusty metal into the trunk, and then she parked the wheelbarrow next to the nail salon. With shaking hands and burning quads, she wrenched the passenger side door open and collapsed into the seat. "You realize you're not going to stop me, right?"

Jewels lifted the armrest and dangled a thick padlock from her pointer finger. "Stop you? I brought help. You didn't think this through the way you did when we chained ourselves to the Nicolson Estate thirty-four years ago, demanding it be labeled a historical site."

Trace wiped the sweat from her brow. She'd forgotten how muggy Florida could be this time of year. Of course, it was nothing compared to the rainforest in Brazil. "I'd forgotten about that."

"You're with friends now. Time to lean on us and stop being on your own. We all know how tough you are. You've got nothing to prove."

But she did. If not to the world then to herself. She'd failed to stop the oil company, and she'd failed to save her intern from drowning. "Thanks. But this isn't your fight."

"If it's your fight, it's our fight. If Wind and Kat were here, they would be by your side, too." Jewels turned onto Main and headed toward Sunset.

"I can't believe that the town council wants my dad's place torn down. They didn't even ask me, and it's on my property."

"How can they do this?" Jewels asked.

"Apparently there's a safety concern with rodents" Trace eyed the clean, proud streets of Summer Island. "Rhonda has to be the ringleader on this. She and Dad used to fight over her right to beach access. She probably thinks if they tear down the house, I'll give up the land."

"Could be. Your home does block her view." Jewels took the next left and barreled down the street, hanging a right into the woods before they reached Trevor's place.

"Yep, remember she convinced my father the county was going to pay him pennies for his land so they could build a road through to connect the main strip with the ocean. He almost sold the property to Rhonda because she'd convinced him that she didn't want to see him leave me with no inheritance."

Jewels gripped the steering wheel like she'd make a ninty degree turn going eighty.

A tractor and bulldozer sat at the edge of the tree line. "Please don't be mad at me for asking this, but do you think Trevor has anything to do with this? It's close to the resort property."

"No. I told you he didn't know that it was your father's house. I think you're being unfair to Dustin. Give him a chance. Once he finds out it's your home and not the shack in the woods, he won't help tear it down."

"Then why hasn't he called back?"

Jewels stopped the vehicle with a jolt.

"Wait! What are you doing? I need to get there before nine."

The car skidded over the loose rocks and shells, but Jewels managed to navigate it back onto the road. "We have thirty minutes. There's still time. If we can stop this with a conversation, we have to try."

Trace reached for the handle, but decided she didn't need a broken ankle from jumping out of a moving vehicle. "I don't like this. Conversation doesn't work." It hadn't worked with Robert. He'd only manipulated her into believing the oil rig followed all mandates and guidelines, but Matt had seen through his charms.

"Trust me. If Dustin doesn't stand down, I'll chain myself to the house with you." Jewels pulled the car to a stop outside the old house that Trevor ran his boat charter business out of.

"One conversation. Then action. Deal?"

Jewels nodded. "Deal."

Fresh air replaced the rust odor, but it didn't help Trace's agitation.

"Remember, Trevor has probably already convinced him

not to tear down the house, so don't go in there with all attitude. It'll only cause damage."

Trace eyed the nearby hotel that appeared to be crumbling almost as much as her father's place. "Fine, but if he touches my home, I'll take that bulldozer to the hotel."

Jewels led Trace around back to the docks, where Trevor tinkered with the powerboat engine. The man worked hard. Trace respected him for that.

"Hi, hon," Jewels called out to Trevor, who dropped what he was doing to pull her into his arms.

For the briefest of moments, Trace wished she had that, but the closest thing she'd ever experienced in her life to a long-term relationship was in the 90s, when she was forced to remain in Antarctica for an extra three weeks when their relief crew came down with the flu. That was awkward since she'd broken up with the guy the day before, thinking they would be moving on.

"I didn't expect to see you here today. I thought the girls were arriving?"

"They are, but you didn't call me back after talking to Dustin."

"I haven't."

Stinging zaps encircled Trace like a giant man o' war hugged her tight. "I told you they were in on it together! That overgrown lionfish is eating away at everything around him," Trace yelled at a shadow that appeared on the other side of the glass sliding door of the house up the hill. "I'm going to stop this, now."

* * *

DUSTIN SIPPED ON HIS COFFEE, eyeing Trace and her BFF warping his friend's mind. He thought about what Trevor had said. Maybe he should go out there and consider having a civil conversation and working things out between them.

His phone buzzed with Rhonda on the screen again. "Hey, what's going on?"

"Word has it that Trace is there and going to pull a stunt to stop the demolition. She's yelling about how it was her daddy's shack. The woman hasn't lived in that home for thirty years. As far as her love for her father, she wasn't even here when he died from a long battle with liver cancer. It's nothing more than a play to beat you, the big-town businessman."

Dustin's gut twisted like one of those sailor knots Trevor was always going on about. "Are you sure? That's cold for anyone to use a family member's death to gain political ground."

"This is the woman who organized a protest in high school against the cafeteria for overuse of plastic," Rhonda said in a holier-than-the-Pope tone.

"Sounds like a reasonable protest."

"Not when she did it because someone else had donated a bunch of cups and plastic silverware to the school and Trace didn't like the attention it brought to a student. The girl rules her life on jealousy. Trust me, don't buy into her games." Rhonda cleared her throat. "You keep your promise to the town. I've rallied votes for your stop order to be terminated as long as you tear down that shack."

"That's the agreement? And I thought big city politics were a mess."

"Listen, I'll head over there to help."

As much as Dustin appreciated the information, he didn't want Rhonda around more than he had to since her mother had basically told him he should marry the woman. He tugged at his ragged T-shirt collar. "Thanks, but I've got this. I appreciate the information and the assist, though. Talk soon." He hung up before she could argue the point.

Dustin grabbed a peach and stepped outside in time for Trace to march up the hill with a glower and groan.

"We didn't know, Trace. But don't worry, I'm sure Dustin will leave your home alone. If the council wants it demolished, he won't do their bidding." Trevor and Jewels stood at Trace's side, ready for a fight.

Dustin slid his shades over his eyes and acted as if he didn't know what they were talking about. He'd learned a long time ago not to give away too much information too quickly in a fight. "What's up?"

"Did you know that what you're about to tear down isn't a shack in the woods, but Trace's home full of her father's belongings?"

He took a chunk out of the fruit; sweet juices trickled down the sides of his mouth and down his chin. He wiped the sticky juice away with the back of his hand and chomped on the peach for a minute before swallowing. "No. I didn't."

"See, I told you." Trevor's shoulders lowered, and Jewels relaxed into his side.

"All is good." Jewels looked to Trace. "Your home's safe."

Trace narrowed her gaze. "No, there's something going on here. I don't trust this six-foot-three eye candy. You better not touch one board on my childhood home."

Dustin had no desire to tear down someone's home, but he couldn't make this that easy for her, not when she held his hotel work orders hostage. "I have to." Dustin took another bite, remaining as nonchalant as possible.

"What?" Trevor shot to the front of the I-hate-Dustin line.

"Don't have a choice. Told the council I would do it, so I have to. You told me not to make them mad before the meeting."

"I thought you realized they were using you to get you to do their dirty work."

"Sure, but I just got off the phone with Rhonda. She's going to rally votes for my stop order to be terminated as long as I tear down that shack. Well, house, I guess. I'm playing nice with the townspeople like you told me to." He had no intention of actually tearing down her home, but she didn't need to know that. He was about to school her on how business really worked.

"You fool." Trace fisted her hands warning Dustin to take a step back. He'd never hit a woman, but that didn't mean he'd let one hit him either. "A one-night stand merits ruining someone's childhood home?"

A level eight eruption of anger burned his chest. "One night?" Dustin threw the peach pit to the ground. "That's what you think? I traded my body for my permit?"

"If the document fits." Trace took a step closer, but Jewels put an arm in front of her.

How could that little whisper of a woman have so much fight? Trace stood nose to chest with him and didn't back down. If he weren't so angry at her manipulative tactics to keep him from working on his hotel, he would respect her. But she'd put the line in the Summer Island beach sand, and he needed to cross it before she took over all his plans.

"Violence isn't the answer," Jewels said in a stand-down tone.

Trevor looked between them. "Whoa, you two. Neutral corners."

Jewels held Trace back with a hand on each shoulder.

"Relax. Let Trevor speak to him. Remember, we're here to talk."

"Listen, man, you can't tear that down. You need to do this for Trace," Trevor said.

Trace cleared her throat, unfurled her fingers, and nudged Jewels out of the way. "Right, we can work this out. We're adults. I'm asking you nicely, don't tear down my house," she said in a honey tone laced with arsenic.

"Too late. Deal's been made. Unless you'll agree to stop fighting me on the renovations to the hotel and support my decision to make changes to the resort." Dustin sauntered past them.

"Never. I won't let the big business bureaucrat win on my home turf. I couldn't fight in Brazil, but I can fight here at home."

He had no idea what she meant, but Dustin marched down the steps without saying anything else. The choice was hers. If the house meant that much to her, she'd agree. If not, Rhonda was telling the truth and Trace never cared about the home, only beating him. "I've got a job to do, and no pretty, sweet-talking woman is going to ruin my chance at fixing up the hotel. Especially when she doesn't even care about that place. She's only doing it to get back at me and prove she can best me. Rhonda said she wasn't even here when her own father passed. That doesn't sound like a woman with strong attachments."

"Give me your keys. I'm done talking," Trace said with malice and murder in her voice.

Jewels reached into her pocket and dropped the keys into Trace's hand. "Dear Lord in heaven, help us."

CHAPTER SIX

TRACE AND DUSTIN about-faced and stomped away like a gun duel at high noon.

She'd fire first.

How dare he come outside looking like a peach-eating Greek God statue with the complex to go with it. The way he stood in his swim trunks, shades, and playboy attitude only irked Trace. That man needed to be busted down a few notches. He reminded Trace too much of that tycoon who played dirtier than his oil spill.

"Dustin, stop," Trevor shrilled like a menopausal woman in the heat.

To Trace's relief, Jewels reached her side. "I'm with you, girl."

Trace didn't pause. Time was too important. Not that she believed the overgrown child would be able to operate a bull-dozer, but she wasn't taking that chance. "You don't have to. I'm not asking you to take my side. I wouldn't do that when your boyfriend is on the opposing team."

"He's not. Trevor's going to stop Dustin. Trust me." Jewels

hopped into the passenger seat and held on to the oh-dear-lord-Trace-is-driving bar.

"You can relax. I won't take a turn on two wheels… this time." She cranked the engine and then backed down the street and hung a right onto the rocky pavement. "Thanks."

Jewels chuckled like a nervous penguin. "No worries. It's only my relationship on the line."

Trace pushed the pedal harder, and they skidded along the rocks and took the final turn to her father's place a little too fast. Too fast to stop when Rhonda stepped out from her oversized, fossil-fuel-farting truck.

"Watch out," Jewels squealed louder than her old drum brakes.

Trace slammed her foot against the pedal and spun three-sixty in a blurry circle of spitting rocks and strangled shouts. The car came to rest with the hood inches from Rhonda and her cross-armed, this-is-war, death-to-the-enemy glower.

Jewels clutched Trace's arm. "Don't let her bait you."

Trace closed her eyes and took in a slow, calming breath to find her inner peace, serene Zen. After two more breaths, she opened her eyes to see an approaching Rhonda wearing a *Team Dustin* printed T-shirt.

Jewels shot from the car. "I knew this was all you. How could you do this to Trace? All for a better view of the ocean."

Trace shot from the car and blocked her advancing friend-turned-crazy-lady. "Wait, no. Don't give her a reason to call the police. Trust me, she'd bring the sheriff and everyone else into her fight. It's pathetic."

The engine, still running behind them, hummed and rattled. The wind through the tree canopy had the leaves whispering their warning, but most of all she heard the sound of heavy equipment starting.

Trace took Jewels by her arm. "There isn't time to waste on her. Come on. This is what she wants."

Trace hopped into the car and pulled around the front of her father's place. The sight of the abandoned, worn structure churned up acid and regrets. No. She couldn't let anyone tear this down. She needed to save her father's place. She had to save something or someone.

Jewels popped the trunk and yanked some chain out. "We need to hurry."

"Not we. Me. I'm not going to let you chain yourself to the house. This is my fight."

Rhonda sauntered toward them, and Trace knew there wasn't time to argue. "Just help me with the chain and then move out of the way."

At the front porch, Trace spotted the cracks and rotted wood of the roof. Inside, the dust was thick and haunting. Everything inside showed like a symbol of her abandonment of her only parent who had raised her. If she had it to do it all over again, she would've come home instead of always fighting the giants who won anyway. Everyone would've been safe if she'd stayed home instead of spending half her life fighting to save the world.

Now wasn't the time to face her demons of past regrets. She opened the cracked front window and slid the chain through to where Jewels took it and walked it to the front door. After three wraps through the house, Trace took her position.

With the padlock in hand, Jewels slid under the chain and stood by her side. "We have you. You're not alone. When the girls arrive, they'll help. Trust me. They might be crazy, but they are the exact crazy we need right now." Jewels slid the lock through the chain and snapped it shut.

In that moment, a war raged inside Trace, knowing that all those years ago she'd left her pregnant high school friend behind to go take on the world. "I'm sorry."

"For what?" Jewels asked.

"For leaving you when you needed me most. I should've stayed in Summer Island. Not just for my father, but for you, too. All these years I was looking for something I never found when I could've been here with you and my dad."

Jewels took her hand and held it tight. "What were you looking for?"

"Purpose," Trace said, the realization knocking the wind from her lungs.

"No. You did what you were meant to do, but you're home now, and I hope you decide to stay."

Stay? She'd never stayed anywhere since she was eighteen. How did one tiny, four-letter word cause heart-palpitating anxiety? Trace forced the panic down and held tight to her best friend. If there was ever a time to stay, it was now. "I'm not leaving this spot. Not today, not tomorrow, not ever as long as there is a threat against my father's place."

* * *

IT HAD BEEN years since Dustin had operated a bulldozer, but it couldn't be that difficult to remember. He climbed in and shut the door. He wouldn't have to tear down her home, because if it meant that much to her, she'd agree to drop the complaint with the city about the historical preservation of the hotel. But if Rhonda was right and she didn't care, she'd stand her ground for no other reason than to beat him. Why else would a town approve an outsider tearing down a building over a native keeping it, unless it was some stunt she was pulling? Considering she was one of those kinds of people who took on causes without reason, he wasn't surprised.

He turned the key in the dozer and let the systems turn on but didn't even check for any warning indicators before he cranked the engines and the vibration churned his nerves into full speed. Too bad the dozer only went at a crawl's pace.

He reached for the parking lever but couldn't find it With a curse, he eyed the new-fangled display in front of him and analyzed it until he located a parking button. Okay, it had been a minute since he'd operated heavy machinery.

Tap. Tap.

Dustin eyed the window and caught a glimpse of Trevor tossing shells at the door.

He waved his arms madly at his side. "Stop. Take a breath. Forget the bet."

He ignored Trevor and located the throttle.

"You're going to make things worse. It's her dad's house," Trevor yelled.

"A home she didn't care about until she found out I wanted to tear it down. It's a power play. Trust me. I know how these things work." He wasn't even sure Trevor could hear him over the sound of the engine, but he pressed the pedal to put the dozer into idle and lifted the levers to engage the joysticks.

"Are you even allowed to operate that thing? The crew will be here any minute. Wait!" Trevor was putting on a good show for Jewels, who had shot him a wrecking glare while she had chased Trace to her car.

"No need to wait." Dustin pulled back the right joystick, lifting the blade. He slid his foot off the pedal and rolled forward but only a few feet before large white trucks pulled up, blocking the only path to the woods.

Great. This gave Trace more time to pull some crazy stunt. He shut everything down and dismounted the dozer. "Come on, men. I'll pay a bonus if you get over there now. Get moving."

The head guy pulled out work orders and flipped through them and then looked at Dustin. "You the owner of the property?"

"No. I'm the one paying, though."

The man tilted his cap up and eyed him and then the paper again.

"County ordered the old shack condemned and torn down," Dustin said in his business tone.

"Right." The man tossed his work orders onto the front seat and directed the men to move their trucks, and he headed to the dozer. "That's more than a shack." The man pointed toward the hotel.

"That's not being torn down," Dustin grunted. "Follow that road, hang a left at the path, and you'll run right into the place."

"Sure? We can knock that place down today, too. No sense in bringing us back later."

Dustin gritted his teeth to keep his train of curses inside and looked to Trevor, who shrugged before he eyed the path through the woods to the shack. No doubt thinking about joining the women with whatever crazy scheme Trace was planning. He knew the type. All about stopping progress in the name of old memories they couldn't let go of to make room for the future. They fought for things they didn't even care about because they didn't have a life.

"You gonna help her thwart my plans? I thought you were the one who wanted me to work on the hotel."

"Yes, but not like this." Trevor remained by his side but

didn't assist with rounding the guys up or expediting their work.

Dustin waved him off like an irritating sand flea. "Don't worry. She's going to back down, and I'll win."

"That's a dangerous game to play."

The bulldozer grumbled to life, and he realized he hadn't heard a sound from the shack area. Dustin set off with Trevor on his heels through the footpath. Dustin worried Trace was lurking somewhere, waiting to pull a stunt, but all was quiet. Quiet couldn't be good.

Worse, she would probably be best buds with the guy in the bulldozer and cry faux tears to win.

At the edge of the woods, he spotted Rhonda, who hot-footed it toward him. Clanking sounded from the front of the house.

"I've already called the sheriff. Don't worry, I'll have them arrested. I'm on *Team Dustin*."

He blinked at Rhonda's printed shirt. His neck heated at his name scribbled across her chest, despite the shade of the trees. "That isn't necessary, really."

Rhonda took him by the hand and walked him to the front of the house.

On the front porch stood Trace and Jewels, hand in hand, chains wrapped across their middles with a lock to secure them.

"I knew you'd pull a stunt like this, Melodramatic Trace." Rhonda tugged Dustin closer to her side, as if claiming him as her possession. His insides churned and he looked to Trevor for help, but his friend only shook his head and shot him a you-did-this-to-yourself grin.

"Name's Tracie. Only my friends call me Trace." She lifted her chin like a military soldier at roll call.

The equipment roared closer. Dustin knew he had to act fast. "Fine, I'll pay you."

"I'm not like you. I can't be bought and sold." She eyed Rhonda's fingers entwined with his. He yanked his hand away, despite knowing she was his only friend in town.

"You're not here because you want to save your father's place. You're only doing this because you want to win."

"Is that what your groupie told you?" Trace looked at him in a way that made him shiver with shame.

No, he wouldn't let her pull his strings like that. The tightness in his chest didn't ease when the town sheriff's car pulled up as he'd expected.

"What's going on here?" The sheriff approached, adjusting his heavy utility belt. "Ah, should've known you two would be at war again. I told my officers that you two in the same town would incite war amongst our locals." He pointed at the *Team Dustin* shirt.

"I don't know about their war, but Trace here—"

"Tracie," she spouted with skin-searing heat in her voice.

"This woman is causing delays in the demolition of this structure that has already been requested and approved by the town."

"Let me guess. You put in the original request." The sheriff eyed Rhonda.

"Town approved," she said in a quick clip.

"Right. Okay, here's how I see it. If this guy wants to be dragged into your feud, that's his stupidity. For now, let's go to neutral corners and fight this out at the town meeting in a couple days."

Dustin stepped forward. "What? You're going to let her get away with obstructing the demolition?"

Rhonda got in the sheriff's face. "Do your job and arrest them."

The sheriff removed his hat with a slow, methodical, powerful movement and glowered down with an authoritative gaze. "You'll be the one arrested if you don't calm down."

She took a step back. "You can't let them get away with this."

Dustin cleared his throat. "I'm with Rhonda on this. Is there nothing I can do to proceed today? They're breaking the law. For the record, I have the paperwork and permission from the town to complete this job. The sign was posted, and all legal measures were taken."

"Were they?" The sheriff plopped his hat back on and marched to his car. "Their property. That's her daddy's place. The place of a friend and former marine brother." He opened his car door. "This is her property legally, and I can't enforce removing her from her own place. And for the record, as long as it is within the bounds of the law, I'm *Team Trace*."

CHAPTER SEVEN

THE NIGHT AIR cooled Trace's stripe of sunburned skin on her arm where the light had cut through the broken section of the roof. She'd lived near the water for her entire life and managed to avoid sun damage until today. Damage that would leave a permanent mark on her nose and cheeks and soul if she lost this battle to keep her father's home from being torn down.

The last ray of light seeped through the trees behind her, and she imagined the green flash announcing the day's end.

As much as she'd urged Jewels to take a break and go home to check on Bri and Houdini, the darkness creeping in around Trace reminded her how alone she truly was in the world. Alone in her guilt.

Crack. Snap. Crunch.

Trace pushed her back against the wall and shimmied to stand, the chains rolling down her body from neck to hips. The constraints were nothing compared to the way she failed a man who gave up everything for her to have a great life.

She took in a deep breath of rust and regrets. "I'm not

leaving, so don't think you'll tear this down in the middle of the night."

"You're moving, but no one's tearing anything down. Not while I'm here."

Trace's friend turned prominent attorney spoke with such authority, the tension in Trace's arms released enough to feel how sore her neck and body were.

"What're you doing here?"

A line of true friends exited the woods. Wind brushed leaves from her hair, Jewels waved, and Kat stomped across the lawn to the front porch.

"Great, first sign of heatstroke is confusion," Kat said.

Trace pushed air into her cheeks like a pufferfish and then blew it out like a whale. "No, we've argued this point for over thirty years. The first sign of a heat stroke is headache."

"Nope, upset stomach." Wind rubbed her belly with one hand and pressed the back of her palm to her forehead with the other. "I should know. I'm suffering heat exhaustion from the walk."

Jewels flipped her hand at Wind like a crossing guard to a speeding car. "Stop. You promised, no complaining."

"I wasn't."

"You were. And we all know that the first sign of heat exhaustion is muscle cramps." Jewels sauntered to Trace, pulled the small key from her pocket, shoved it into the padlock, and turned. The arm snapped free and the chains loosened, but Trace held them tight to make sure they didn't fall to the ground.

She scanned the tree line. "What if *Team Dustin* shows again?"

Wind slid a finger under her right eye and swiped some

melting black mascara goo from her bottom lid. *"Team Dustin?"*

"Yeah. She printed a shirt that said that and strutted around here like a peacock in mating season." Trace smacked her lips, trying to alleviate dryness on her tongue.

Kat grabbed the chain and tugged. "Get out of there. You need a break. Jewels, you take her back to your place and get her some food."

"Not leaving my post. If Dustin catches sight of me, he'll mow over this place."

Kat unfurled her fingers, and the chain dropped to the ground. "I'm here now."

"Hey, what about me? I didn't walk over here to look pretty," Wind said in a breezy tone.

Kat turned to Wind, arms and attitude crossed. *"We'll* be here. As a matter of fact, Wind offered to take your place."

"What? Me?" Wind flipped her hair. "Nope. Not happening. I'm not a fighter." She eyed her nails. "Besides, I just got a manicure. I can't damage the polish on that death rope. You do it."

"I'm going to go fight with the county. I've already got a meeting set up over the sale of my parents' estate, so that'll get me in the door." Kat cracked her knuckles. "I'll stop this legally."

"Can you do that?" Wind shrugged and then tip-toed up the front porch like a fairy in a ballet. "If so, I'm happy to stand guard for Trace."

"No. It's my fight. I'll stand guard."

Jewels nudged Trace a step farther from the chains and then slid them up around her own middle and snapped the lock into place. "I'll stay. Wind, you take Trace to eat. Kat will go see if she can do anything to help legally. Although I'm sure the offices are already closed for today. If so, you can return to my place and send Wind over in a few hours to do her shift."

Kat pushed up her sleeves. "I'll take the watch after that."

Trace shook her head and touched Wind's silky, impractical sleeve. "You don't have to do that. I'll take a break for an hour and then return."

Wind's face softened. Her right eyebrow lifted in encouragement, and the left side of her mouth drooped with disappointment. A battle between filler and Botox ensued in a strange war of emotions. "No. I'll take my shift. What are Friendsters for?" She winked. "I might need to borrow something to wear that rust stains won't ruin. I'm sure you have something."

Kat huffed. "Who asked you to wear stilettos and silk to a sandy, buggy, outdoor beachside fight?"

"When Jewels said we needed to help Trace with a fight, I assumed a cocktail party to save the dolphins."

Jewels laughed with a lightness that drew everyone's attention. "Seriously? Since when does Trace do parties and social events? You should've known to bring a flashlight and bolt cutters to any Trace occasion."

Kat nodded her agreement, and Trace shrugged. "Can't argue with that. How did you not know that, Wind? Trust me, you're better off in the theater and theatrics than conservation and crime." She toed at a beetle climbing a stick. "Besides, trust me when I say all of you should let me handle this. I don't want to drag you guys into anything that isn't your fight."

Wind slid her arm around Trace and squeezed tight. "If it's your fight, it's our fight. We're more than Friends. We're sisters."

For a second, Trace wished that they'd been around on the oil rig, because they would've snapped her out of the trance Robert Remming had her in and then Matt would've survived.

"Good. You can take the midnight shift," Kat said over her shoulder before she reached the trail toward the main road.

"Midnight? I need my beauty sleep," Wind shouted after her.

"Bring a pillow." Kat disappeared beyond the tree line, and Trace looked to Jewels, standing behind the chains.

Guilt sucked the fight out of Trace. "I can't ask you to betray Trevor like this. I don't want to be the cause of a fight between you two."

"Don't worry about that. Trevor and I are fine. Besides, I've known Trevor for months. I've known you for almost all my fifty years. Now go get some rest."

Trace stood eyeing her father's house and wishing she could do more, but Jewels was right. Exhaustion was taking hold, and she needed some rest if she was going to keep fighting.

"Thanks. You ladies are the best friends any woman could ever ask for in her life. Even if I don't deserve it." Her mumbles slipped out, but to her relief, none of her friends acknowledged them. She shuffled through the woods and decided to walk to the main road to avoid crossing behind Trevor's house so she didn't have to chance running into Dustin.

"Hey, hold up. Woman in heels here." Wind ran on her toes to catch Trace at the edge of the road. "I don't know how all this got so out of hand. I'm going to go speak with Dustin after we get you fed and in bed."

Trace fought the twinge of jealousy that she'd felt each time she'd seen Wind with Dustin. Why? She had no clue. The man was impossible. "No. I don't want to strain any more relationships." She nearly choked on her last word.

Wind grabbed onto Trace's shoulder to slow her down. "Dustin was a distraction while I was here for a while. Nothing more. I'd never choose him over my friends."

Trace didn't have a chance to argue before they spotted Dustin, Trevor, Rhonda, and marine shop owner Skip on Main Street. All of them huddled together outside the courthouse, but there was no sign of Kat.

Her pulse quickened. She wanted to race across the road and pick a fight with them here and now instead of waiting for the county to decide. No way the county would ever agree to tear down her home. It had been some sort of backchannel, slip-through-the-cracks Rhonda tactic that had let it even get this far. Before Trace could form her words to go speak to them, Wind abandoned Trace's side and marched across the road.

Horns blared and cars swerved. Trace held her breath until Wind and her dramatics made it safely across the street. Dustin looked like a suicidal squirrel eyeing an escape route through traffic. His hands shot up in front of him, but Trace couldn't hear a word they were saying from her side of the road.

Once the one town light changed, she made her way across the street, eyeing the flyers Rhonda passed out to each stopped car. One of them caught a breeze and landed a few steps away. Trace picked it up. The headline read: *Rats, Roaches, and Rabid Rodents Take Over Summer Island.*

A picture of her father's house from an angle that made the structure look dilapidated and abandoned drove the point into the heart. Underneath the awful picture and loaded headline, it rambled on about the safety of their island and home prices and town pride, all pointing at the one eyesore of their community. It was a call for votes to have the county take over land that had been neglected after the passing of one of their own. A man who cared about his community. And the failure of his daughter to take care of his legacy made it a town problem.

Trace crumpled the paper into her fists, but before she could have words with the childhood enemy turned adult villain, Wind snagged her by the hand and yanked her away.

"What are you doing? I need to stop this garbage being distributed."

Wind didn't listen. She only hightailed it across to Jewels's house. "Can you believe that man? I'm going to take him down. This is personal now."

"Now?" Trace lifted both her brows. "Ah, always been personal."

"Right. Of course." Wind kicked off her shoes and snagged her pink and purple suitcase with an image of one of her shows tattooed to the outside of it. "I mean that this isn't only about the land and property. It isn't motivated by what's right. It's motivated out of a sick stick-it-to-the-friends-who-never-accepted-me cause. A cause Rhonda chose to start in middle school when she drew a literal line in the sand and told me not to cross it. Oh, I'm crossing now. How can a grown-up be so immature? I'm gonna pull her mousy, greasy hair from her head."

"Yep, that's the mature way to handle it." Trace plopped down on the couch, the fight fleeing her body for a moment in exchange for resting her swollen feet and aching back.

"She wants to play dirty? I'm going to get some mud." She slid on some flats, grabbed her purse and keys, and headed for the door. "Oh, sorry. You'll be okay here, right? I mean, you can get something to eat and all?"

"Yes, but where are you going?"

Wind stormed into the kitchen.

Houdini heard the call and raced into the room. He scurried up onto the couch, her secret letter in his mouth.

Trace's throat went Mojave Desert dry. She grabbed hold and glowered at him until he released it. She collapsed back and tucked the letter under her hip. She needed to find a new hiding spot or shred or burn it.

"It's time to get the townspeople on *Team Trace*," Wind said before downing a glass of water.

Exhaustion took hold, and Trace closed her eyes. Houdini took it as an engraved invitation for lap time. She welcomed his soft fur between her fingers and his therapeutic, relaxing purr. "No. I don't want this to be a town problem. I only want to let Kat work her magic and save my dad's place. She'll be back soon with good news, I'm sure of it."

Wind's phone played some Broadway song, causing Trace to open her eyes.

Houdini coiled into a ball and snored.

"Really? According to the text Kat just sent, we'll need to be present at the town meeting tomorrow if you want to keep your house and land. Apparently Rhonda has a development company in her back pocket willing to pay big money for her property, but the county would need to extend the road through your land. They'll offer fair market value for the property."

Trace shot up, nervous energy pushing aside her body-crying, toe-swelling, back-aching exhaustion. "That can't be true. They don't have the right. I just won't sell."

"I don't trust Rhonda. I'm sure she has another plan to

make this happen, even if you refuse to sell. I'm not going to stay here and let her win. Trust me. I'll take care of this. *Team Trace* will win."

She didn't get a chance to argue with Wind, who slammed her glass on the counter and took off on a rampage. Wind on a rampage was like a stiletto-wearing bull in a porcelain factory.

CHAPTER EIGHT

"I'M NOT WEARING THAT." Dustin refused to even touch the purple T-shirt with *Team Dustin* written in swirly letters. Not even after the warnings Rhonda had whispered in his ears before she finally left Trevor's house last night, not even after this morning when she showed up with coffee, coaxing conversation, and not even when she'd returned for a free meal. Nope. No way he'd ever wear that girly billboard.

Trevor's house wasn't big enough for Rhonda's drama, Trevor's evil looks, and his peace.

Rhonda sighed like a two-year-old forced to stand in a line at Disney World. "You want to win, don't you?"

"Win? You make it sound like we're playing a game." Dustin huffed and abandoned the too-small table he'd been forced to eat at knee-to-knee with Rhonda.

Trevor fled the few paces to the kitchen, but not without a comment. "I'm with Dustin. Let's keep things civil. This is her father's home, right?"

"Civil?" Rhonda screeched like a seagull with a head cold. "You think they'll be civil? They're going around town soliciting votes for the meeting. If you don't work harder, they'll win."

"Win what?" Trevor grumbled. "It's her house. It should be her decision."

"Correction. Father's house. A house she abandoned along with her so-called family the minute she could leave to go pull stunts that would cost millions of dollars to large companies."

Dustin shifted between his guilt at tearing down any home and his desire not to cave for an exhausting, stubborn Trace who, according to Rhonda, only cared about winning and nothing about her father's legacy. "Let's just go to the meeting, behave like professionals, and we should be fine. The only thing I care about is getting that stop order removed. If she'll agree to that, she can keep her father's home."

"Don't you go goody-boy on me. We had a deal. You tear down that house, and I get that injunction lifted."

Heat surged over Dustin's skin. "I originally agreed to tear down the shack. I didn't know you meant her home. You misled me."

"Miscommunicated," she huffed with a nostril flare. "You owe me. I took on your problem, and you promised to have my back."

Trevor shot an I-told-you-you're-an-idiot smile at Dustin.

Dustin gritted his teeth and took his dish to the kitchen. "I didn't realize it was blackmail."

"It's not." Rhonda flipped her tone faster than a dinghy capsized in a storm. "You don't know the women the way I do." She pushed her shoulders back, extending her *Team-Dustin*-covered breasts out. "They are the evil ones here, not me. I'm only trying to help. It's because of Trace that my father's business shut down—due to one of her so-called protests. She not only ended his career but my parents' marriage. Trust me. Don't believe a word that woman says."

Dustin took a breath and willed himself not to ask, but he was a man of facts when it came to business. "How did she put your father's company out of business?"

The shade of hell didn't describe the color change in Rhonda's face. "She told everyone in town he was harming the environment with his pesticides. That he single-handedly drove away the bee population that provided honey and nutrients to our local plants. Jewels jumped on board and even created some blob of clay that was supposed to resemble a honeycomb that was placed in some glass box on display."

Dustin remembered Trevor mentioning something about that a few months ago when he first started dating Jewels. "I understand. That's why I spent all night going over the historical zoning laws and presenting a new development plan to the county." He flipped his wrist to discover they only had a few minutes before they had to leave. "I need to go shower and shave. We'll meet you there in twenty."

Rhonda side-stepped, blocking his exit from the living area toward the stairs to the only indoor shower. "Remember, you let them get away with not tearing down that shack, and you won't ever win your fight for the hotel."

The heat from her attitude seared his disposition. He wouldn't let anyone, not even Rhonda, overstep when it came to his business. "I know you want that house torn down for a view and that you're using me to get that done. I'll do what I can to help your cause since you've tried to help me, but I won't be bullied into it."

"Bullied?" She laughed like a ferret on helium. "I'm not the bully. Remember that. If you allow them to win on one count, they'll win on all of them. Don't complain to me when you lose the war, because I've warned you. That's all I can do. I'm the good witch in this story."

Dustin remained standing there even after the door slammed behind an infuriated Rhonda.

Trevor dried a glass and slammed it down on the counter. "You better decide how far you want to take this. That woman might be your only friend left if you tear down Trace's house without a good reason."

"I thought you were my friend."

"I am, and that's why I'm being honest. You'll never forgive yourself if you destroy Trace's father's house." Trevor picked up another glass and stuck the cloth through the mouth and twisted side to side. "Jewels says this isn't just about her father's house. Something happened to her. Something she's not talking about."

"What?" Dustin's skin crawled at the thought. He wanted to win but not harm Trace. That's why he'd spent all night reviewing the zoning laws. If he could keep her home and not give in to her demands, he'd be the bigger man.

"Don't know. I'm just saying. She doesn't want to give in to the hotel remodel for a reason more than we understand."

Dustin grabbed his proposal from the coffee table. "Remember, you're the one who begged me to come live here with you."

"I know, but I never thought it would turn south, catch the trade winds, and end up in Cuba before you even started." Trevor put that glass down next to the other clean one. "All I'm saying is that I'm *Team Dustin*, as long as the leader doesn't play dirty. And if I know my friend, he'd never destroy someone's home to get a few shutters updated on a building."

"I'm not evil. But Trace brings out the worst in me. I had to deal with so many tree huggers in business, I'm sick of them. All bark and no real cause."

Dustin hot-footed it up the stairs, showered, shaved, and studied his situation. If he betrayed Rhonda, he could alienate his only friend besides Trevor. If he chose Trace's side, he could lose Rhonda, the only one who was willing to take his side on his problem with the county.

After sulking and thinking for the little time he had left, he joined Trevor to head out to the town meeting. Nerves swam and spun in his gut. "I've been thinking. I'll do what I can to not tear down Trace's house if the county approves these new plans. No reason to bite the head off a shark if I can stay on land."

Trevor laughed. "I'm not sure that made sense to most people, but to me it does. I've got your back in there if that's the case." He slapped Dustin on the shoulder. "Thanks for not making me choose sides."

"I won't unless they do. Besides, the T-shirt thing was never an idea I agreed with. That was all Rhonda. I doubt a few shirts will change anything around here anyway."

They turned the corner and spotted a congregation of people standing outside the main courthouse. All of them were dressed in hot pink shirts. A nip of nerves ate at him.

"What's going on?" Dustin asked rhetorically.

Trevor opened his mouth, but he didn't have to answer when they reached the front walk and Trace turned to show off her bedazzled, beguiling, billboard of a cause on her chest. White swirly letters with stones and glitter that spelled out *Team Trace* gnawed at his resolve. "What's this?"

Wind pushed through the crowd and flipped her hair over her shoulder. "You didn't think we'd let you take down her childhood home, did you?"

"Considering you took turns chained to the shack? The thought never even floated to the surface." Dustin spotted Rhonda waving a shirt at him from the other side of the crowd. A crowd that made him believe they were waiting for a rock concert more than a town hall meeting.

He looked down his nose at the little blonde who threatened his hotel for no reason but spite. In an attempt to remember they were enemies, he reminded himself that she wasn't a beautiful, sweet woman, despite her petite frame and blonde hair. But then he remembered Trevor's words about how she was struggling with something and swallowed his pride. "You need to calm down so we can work this out."

Trace rose to her toes. "Now you want to talk to me? Funny how your attitude changed when you know you're going to lose."

Jewels slid between them. "Now children, why don't we talk—"

That all-too-familiar competitive slap in the face stung his resolve to be cordial. "I don't lose."

Trace pointed to the crowd. "You're going to."

Trevor appeared at their side, the crowd pushing them around. "Come on, you two. We need to talk about how to work it out instead of allowing everyone else to stir up more trouble."

The front door swung open, and out stepped Cap. "Calm it down out here. Anyone not being cordial will be escorted from the building, right Sheriff?"

A man Dustin hadn't met, standing in a police uniform of shorts and button-up dark top, waved his hat at the crowd. The slight young officer didn't look like he could handle a mob like this one.

The people funneled in.

At the doorway, Trace leaned into Dustin's side. "You can back down before you're humiliated."

Rhonda tossed shirts into the crowd, and Dustin snagged the gaudy purple, swirly, girly shirt. He ripped off his coat and slid the shirt over his head. The too-tight fabric hugged his chest and stomach like a woman's Spanx. "We'll see who wins."

CHAPTER NINE

TRACE SETTLED between Jewels and Wind but didn't see Kat anywhere. Mr. Mannie hobbled in with his pink *Team Trace* T-shirt on. As ridiculous as this was, it warmed Trace's heart that he was taking her side. But behind him stood Skip, clad in a *Team Dustin* uniform. The room was dotted with bright shirts scattered like a rainbow had spewed rabid rose-colored rabbits and predatory purple panadas.

That was it. No more of Wind's cocktail creations. Trace rubbed her head, not sure if it was from last night's drink or the stress of her friends and family feuding. "This isn't right. The town shouldn't be torn apart because I want to save my father's house."

Jewels rubbed her arm with an I-know hitch to her brow.

Wind shot forward. "Don't go soft on me, girl. You're in the right."

"Am I? Rhonda's right about one thing. I wasn't here when my father died."

Jewels pulled her in for a friend group hug with Wind.

"Your father didn't tell you until it was too late. You couldn't make it on time. That isn't your fault."

"Maybe not, but I could've handled things differently. I was always off protecting everything instead of staying home to protect my father. I should've done more."

Wind slid free, eyeing the town residents around them, but Jewels's gaze landed firmly on Trace. "When you're ready."

Trace ignored the offer. Not now. Not here. Not ever.

Mrs. Whitmore marched up, pumping her arms and waggling her butt like she did when she powerwalked up the street for her daily exercise. "You're gonna win this. No way the county can vote against their own." She adjusted her water belt she wore everywhere out of the house. "Then again, Rhonda's a native, too." She eyed her shirt and then Rhonda.

Wind stood and shot out her hand. "We thank you for your help. Especially when we're attempting to preserve the past of our town elders instead of tearing down their memories for condos."

"Condos?" Mrs. Whitmore tugged her shirt down and pushed out her sagging chest. "*Team Trace* all the way!" She pumped her fist into the air and then powerwalked to the front of the room.

"Where's Kat?" Trace asked the question that had been haunting her since after breakfast when Kat had sped out of the house with only a backhand wave and promise to save the town.

"There she is." Wind pointed to the side door where the town council entered with her.

They all took their seats, Kat included.

"What's going on?" Trace fidgeted with her shirt hem and her anxiety.

"Probably pulling some lawyer stunt." Wind cupped the side of her mouth and hollered, *"Team Trace!"*

Those two words tossed fuel on the town debate fire, and the room erupted in boisterous debate.

A gavel pounded against the laminated top of the long table at the front of the room that was packed to the brim with residents.

"I haven't seen a turnout like this for one of these meetings since the great debate of Greg Yates and his eligibility to run for mayor." Jewels scanned the room as if working an ops mission for Summer Island Secret Security.

"Why was that a thing?" Wind asked in a this-sounds-deliciously-intriguing tone.

"He was born in another country but had been a citizen for years. His opponent stated he wasn't legal because he wasn't born here."

"In the United States?" Trace asked, more to say something so she could ignore the twisting, turning, tumultuous waves in her stomach.

"No, Summer Island." Jewels half smiled. "If that kept Mr. Yates's from winning, I'm sure we can use prejudice against *Team Dustin.*"

Trace rubbed her belly. She'd used some underhanded stunts to win against big business before, and she didn't respect what Dustin was trying to do, but he was a victim, too. Rhonda could be persuasive enough to convince anyone they were in the right. She let out a long I've-been-stupid sigh and wanted to go talk to Dustin, to work things out, but when the gavel hit the tabletop three more times and the shouts still didn't stop, she knew it was too late to work it out between themselves. The town wanted a say now.

"Everyone, please." Mayor Maclin stood with hands

splayed toward the audience. "We won't accomplish anything this way."

People quieted. A few rogue shouts echoed through the silence. "Stop erasing elders!" Mrs. Whitmore shouted.

Trace was impressed with her word choice for impact. Maybe she'd underestimated her ally.

"Rats, roaches, and vagrants be gone!" Skip shouted in a voice aged with smoke, years, and attitude

"All of this is useless because the law will dictate what happens. That's why we have a special announcement with Kathryn Stein."

"She's one of them." Rhonda shot from her chair to the front.

Trace gave Kat credit. She didn't even flinch at an advancing, riotous Rhonda.

"I'm on the side of the law. You may sit down, or you may be removed from this room," Kat said with her authoritative attorney attitude.

"You can't do that." Rhonda turned to the people watching. "She's not even a local any longer."

"Actually, I am. I'm owner of my parents' home. I bought it the other day. A home I grew up in, learned in, played in."

Rhonda rounded on her, but Sheriff Vincent slipped to Rhonda and took hold of her arm before whispering something in her ear. She gave him a sideways taser-stinging stare but then settled into her seat in the purple section.

"Now, if we may proceed." Mayor Maclin took her position in the center of all and moved the mic to speak. "We have a proposition that will be within the confines of the law and will hopefully satisfy both sides of this issue. Ms. Stein has graciously drawn up contracts that both parties will sign. In this contract, the following will be executed."

The mayor shuffled some papers but not fast enough that Trace missed her shaking fingers. What was she about to announce? Certainly Kat wouldn't have helped them with tearing down Trace's home. No. She'd never do that.

Mayor Maclin placed her palms flat against the table and cleared her throat. "Due to the complaint filed against the property located at Latimer Circle by a resident—"

"Go Rhonda," someone shouted from the back.

Mayor Maclin shot a warning stare over the crowd that Trace had no doubt reached her target. "After having an inspector review the property, it was determined that the building was not up to code and it did present a risk to the town."

"What?" Wind shot up. This time it was Kat who shot a look and nailed Wind into silence.

"Several official warnings were sent to the residence with no response. Therefore the town approved demolition."

Mr. Mannie slammed the butt of his cane twice against the linoleum floor. "She didn't receive none. How crooked is this town?"

"However," the mayor continued, "it was determined that the mail was not forwarding to the appropriate heir to the property. Once contact was made, the property owner has expressed interest in bringing the home up to code."

"Yes, I would be happy to do that. Thank you," Trace blurted, her heart, pulse, and grief slowing to starfish pace.

"No. She had her chance." Skip rose her hands, pumping the crowd into disorder.

Mr. Mannie slammed his fist against the table, drawing attention to the usually serene person. "There's more that might interest all parties if people would behave like adults long enough to hear it. We're done with this town feud."

Dustin stood, his eyes darting about the room, skimming Trace but never settling on her. "Sir, can I ask about my property? Will I have an opportunity to share my new plans that will meet with all county and city historical zoning standards so that the stop work order can be lifted?"

Trace was so relieved that her home wouldn't be torn down, she wanted to make things right for once in her life. To stop fighting for things that weren't her battle. "I'm willing to withdraw my complaint if he'll meet the historical criteria specified by the town ordinances."

"We have decided that the restoration of the hotel is important to the town," Mayor Maclin stated flatly, but that palm of hers shot up again like a wall to stop any further conversation. "The issue is that we don't have the staff right now to monitor the progress to make sure that Trace Latimer's house is brought up to code, nor the ability to watch over Mr. Dustin Hawk and his hotel project. Our fear is that Trace Latimer won't have the ability or construction know-how to make the necessary changes; however, she possesses the information to update the structure while remaining true to the wants and needs of our town."

"I can manage," Trace blurted, but it was as if her voice was blocked by the silver chia-pet hair in front of her.

"Dustin Hawk has the construction experience to make the changes to his hotel but lacks the knowledge of what is within the zoning laws."

"I've studied them. I know the laws," Dustin said loud and proud.

"Sir, what is the allowed paint color for shutters, and are you allowed to remove the bay window at the front?"

Dustin lifted his chin. "I'll keep the bay window as is. The paint colors I have on my spreadsheet."

"Wrong. The bay window must be removed," Trace grumbled too loud, drawing attention to her.

"That's correct, Ms. Latimer," Mayor Maclin announced. "This is why you both will work together to restore both properties in the image of what is appropriate for Summer Island. Ms. Latimer will sign off on all paperwork at his hotel, and Mr. Hawk will instruct and sign off on all structural changes to her home. Each party must finance their own costs but will be monitored and assisted by the other person."

Trace's gut wrenched tight. Her pulse thrummed. "That doesn't make sense. We can both do our own work. He's not standing over me every time I screw a nail into a wall."

"Hammer," Dustin said tugging at the too-tight T-shirt he wore. "What I mean is that I agree with Ms. Latimer. We'll be fine on our own."

The room erupted, Rhonda leading the charge, with shouts of elections and impeachment. The mayor set her gavel down, folded her hands, and waited. Waited for Rhonda to have her tantrum. Waited for the shouts to calm. Waited for Trace and Dustin to face each other and their fate.

When the crowd finally quieted, Mayor Maclin rose from her seat and spoke in her political, parental voice. "I want you all to leave here thinking about your behavior and actions. We are a proud and passionate town. That's one of the things I love about all of you. But sometimes following a cause can be counterproductive. I encourage each of you to look around. Mrs. Whitmore, last week you were almost hit with a fine for your lawn being too tall. Pat O'Rilley mowed it for you in the heat of the evening after working all day. And Mr. O'Reilly, last year, when you fell from the ladder and couldn't take your cans to your street, Jewels Boone made sure they were out on time every week for trash day. None of you filed complaints against each other. You helped your neighbors because we're not just neighbors, we're a family. A Summer Island family."

The crowd, shamed into silence, watched the town council end the meeting and disappear through the side door. But Trace wasn't happy. This wasn't the ending she had hoped for. The thought of working side by side with Dustin Hawk churned her stomach and heart into a whirlpool of fear. Fear that she would kill the guy by the time they were done working together. Fear that she didn't have fight enough left in her to make sure he kept his promise with preserving the history of the hotel. Fear that spending that much time with a handsome, charismatic man would twist her resolve and make her believe in possibilities—the possibility that he wasn't the big business, bureaucratic boy toy she thought him to be. She knew what could happen when you joined forces with someone like him. He'd take her trust and twist it until she broke.

CHAPTER TEN

THE TOWN HALL emptied faster than Dustin had fled Seattle for a less hectic life—a life that was anything but simple.

Rhonda cut him off at the edge of the curb outside of the courthouse. "You're not giving up, are you? You've got money. Hire your own lawyer. That woman works for Trace and her gang."

Dustin rubbed his head trying to alleviate the headache he thought he'd left behind in corporate America. "Lawyers take time and money. I'm sure Kat did this case pro bono."

"Bone what?"

"Never mind." He shuffled forward, wanting to find some quiet, but Rhonda wasn't going to allow that.

"I thought I chose a winner." Rhonda maneuvered in front of him, arms and attitude crossed in front of him. "I thought you had a spine. You're nothing more than a jellyfish."

"Original. Really. I hate the ocean and I understood that cliché." Dustin looked to Trevor, smiling as he stood with the ladies on the other side of the road. It looked happier on their side. "As you said, I'm a businessman, and that means I know when to work with someone and when to fight them. I achieved what I wanted to here today. The stop order has been lifted."

"What did I get? That dilapidated building remains an eyesore, and it's blocking my future. I need that land."

Dustin took in a deep breath and knew in that moment he had to choose to either continue placating Rhonda or to tell her the truth that she didn't have a prayer to legally beat Trace. "The land isn't mine to give."

Rhonda turned all shades of angry and thrust her arms down at her sides. "You can get it for me, though. I won't let you give up. We're in this together. We'll fight her with delays until the town forces the place to be demolished. It's what you want, right? Our project to move forward, a beautiful area for your guests and me to enjoy?"

"Yes. No." Dustin didn't want to hurt the woman who'd tried to help, even if she was misguided and ruthless. He guessed the poor woman had always wanted to be a member of the Trace friend group but was never invited so she lashed out and had never stopped, despite thirty-plus years.

"Which is it?"

"As I said, it isn't mine to give. And it never will be. I won't play dirty to push a person from their home. I'm sorry."

Rhonda spun in a dust storm of salty air and curses. "Coward." She was madder than he'd ever seen a woman. And he'd made plenty mad in his past.

"I have money and time invested in this. I won't let you give up."

"I'll reimburse you for the T-shirt printing." Not that he'd ever wanted the darn shirts in the first place.

"You owe me more than that." Rhonda stormed off.

He knew that wouldn't be the last he'd hear from her. But

for now, he decided it was time to face Trevor and the women and the fact that he'd be working with the one woman he knew he'd want to throw in the ocean within the first five minutes.

After two horn honks, a shout from a *Team Trace* supporter, and heatstroke, Dustin managed to cross the street, tugging his arms out of his coat. Sweat pooled at his lower back. His heart beat in his temples.

"Don't make me regret this." Kat shoved a legal-sized envelope into his chest. "Documents to sign off for you."

Trace already clutched an envelope of her own to her stomach as if to keep from hurling her breakfast at the thought of working with him. "Looks like we're going to be a team," she said with a sagging, politically correct smile.

"Guess so." Dustin shifted between his Italian leather shoes.

"Get changed and meet at my house." Trace's smile turned to military straight-lined lips.

"Your house? Why there?" Dustin had no desire to run into Rhonda again today. He was scared she'd throw him over the retaining wall into the canal.

"You didn't think we'd start with the hotel," Trace huffed. She whirled on Kat, who didn't even flinch. The woman was stronger than a president in a political debate. "I told you he'll never work with me. What were you thinking?"

Kat looked between them before she pulled another sheet out of her burgundy designer briefcase. "I figured that would be an issue for you both."

Trace glanced over the itemized schedule. "Mornings at the hotel and afternoons at my house?"

"Yes." Kat gave a curt nod.

"Why not the other way around?" He knew Rhonda would

be doing her morning walk and didn't want to run into her when he didn't have to.

"Because there isn't shade at the hotel to work under in the afternoons. There's plenty of shade near Trace's place."

"Looks like Kat thought of everything." Jewels held tight to Trevor with a look of relief soothing the tension around her crow's feet.

"I'll go change, grab my ladder and tools, and then we can start on the sagging roof of the porch since it's a hazard."

"No. We'll start with the support beams. That's the bigger issue."

Kat slid another piece of paper from her briefcase and handed a copy to each. "You'll start by clearing everything out of the first room you'll be working on at the hotel and the house. After that, you'll work systematically down this list. You'll see where permits need to be filed and when inspections must be completed."

Trace scanned the list. "Where will we put all the stuff when we clear it out? It's going to get ruined if furniture and stuff are left outside."

Wind pointed to the starred item at the bottom.

"You'll store it all in the hotel rooms you're not actively working in." Wind laughed. "Leave it to Kat. She's got everything categorized and organized."

Trace glanced over the paper at Dustin as if to confirm that he agreed to it. "That means we'll have to carry all the stuff from her house through the woods to the hotel. That's a lot of unnecessary work. We should get a storage bin delivered or put a tarp over everything."

"A tarp? Sure." She shoved the extra papers in her envelope, and her eyes went wide and wild. "Let's throw all my father's belongings out into the elements and forget about them like we should forget about the history of the hotel." She narrowed her gaze at him as if to pinpoint the best place to strike him down. "Don't think you're going to cut corners while I'm involved. I won't allow you to break laws, twist truths, and disregard all that's important to save a little cash and hard labor." Her small pointer finger jabbed him in the chest. "You've got just as much—if not more—to lose as I do."

"Or I could just sell the hotel and be done with all this," he blurted.

Trace's expression turned from combative to content. Her long, dark eyelashes framing her ocean blue eyes fluttered. The corners of her mouth jerked upward into a bone-chilling angle. "You can't run from this fight. No one wants that hotel. You'll never be able to sell it unless you fix it up. The only way you're going to get it fixed up is by doing what I say. And I say we're following Kat's list and doing things right." She turned on her heels and marched away with a sway of her hips, bounce of her hair, and stomp of desperation.

That woman was passionate. A fighter for all. All except the ones she couldn't even see needed her dedication instead of her disdain. And he wanted to know why Trace Latimer hated him. Why, since the day they met, he could sense a connection with her yet they were still on opposing sides.

CHAPTER ELEVEN

THE SEARING HEAT of the afternoon sun boiled the air into steam inside Trace's childhood home. She'd forgotten what it was like living with no air conditioning.

"You sure you don't want our help?" Wind asked, despite backstepping toward the doorway.

Kat adjusted her suit jacket. How the woman still looked put together in this heat was beyond Trace's comprehension. "I'll come back after my meeting at my parents' house to check to make sure you and Dustin haven't murdered each other."

Jewels stuck out her hand like they were twelve. "Sisters unite."

Everyone eyed the invitation of childhood bonding, but no one moved except the frog that croaked in the corner and hopped around after flies.

Trace rolled her eyes, but deep down she wanted this moment. The moment where they all bound together to face anything in life. A childhood promise to put each other first before parents or boys or life. She shot her arm out and covered Jewels's hand. "Sisters unite."

Kat's heels clicked against the old hardwood floor. Her hand covered Trace's with strength and comfort. She always knew these women would have her back, but would they feel the same if they knew the truth of her actions in Brazil?

The frog ribbited its agreement.

Wind laughed and glided across the floor with her long dress fluttering behind. "Sisters unite."

They all giggled like schoolgirls in a simple time when the only worries they had were when to swim or sleep.

"I'll be around if you need me." Jewels led the gaggle of women out of the house, leaving Trace standing in the center of the one main room eyeing the clutter.

Before she could face the work, she slid from her pocket the envelope she'd retrieved from her hiding place in the guest room of Jewels's place and opened the desk drawer. At least here, Houdini couldn't steal it to show the world. That little rascal loved drama.

She popped open the hidden compartment. To her surprise, inside sat a wrapped box with a note.

Trace picked it up and slid the envelope into its spot before closing the hiding place up. The note only said *To Trace* in her father's scribble. She brushed the words with her fingers, imagining him sitting at his desk writing this to her.

She pulled the tape, already surrendering from the humidity, free and slid the box from the paper. Inside she found a copy of *Anne of Green Gables*. Not any copy. The one from her childhood. The one she'd received on her eleventh birthday from her dad.

Same worn corners and faded cover. She opened the flap and found a new message inside.

To my dearest daughter,

I'm sorry I'm not there for your fiftieth birthday, but I hope this book reminds you of how much I love you. The way Mathew loved Anne. A man ill-equipped at raising a daughter but who did his best and always wanted her to be free of her insecurities and find her place in the world. I'm so happy you found your place. I'm so proud of you. I hope you can forgive me for not telling you I was leaving this world, but I couldn't interrupt your charge to make this world a better place.

Your proud and loving father,

Dad

Tears fell down her cheeks. "I'm not that girl, Dad. I failed. I failed you. I failed myself. I failed Matt. I'm sorry for not being better."

Why had she left? She'd had an amazing childhood. Her father had given her freedom, independence, and love.

The air hung with a haze of dust and regrets.

Steps outside crunched branches and kicked shells, warning of someone approaching. She flipped her wrist over to see the time on the dive watch that her father had given her as a parting gift all those years ago. Crusty matter ate away at the inside, and it hadn't kept time well for years, but she had never bought a new one.

She shook off the memories, wiped her tears away, and focused on the task at hand. Reprimanding the rude Dustin Hawk for being late.

Shocker.

The front porch creaked.

"How long does it take to put on old clothes and get over here? It's been an hour." Trace placed the book from her father on the bookshelf and turned to see Dustin move into sight.

His usual flirtatious lopsided grin and attention-provoking strut turned to a crumpled old man who looked like he'd swallowed a lemon. "I had a few calls to make. You could've started without me," Dustin grumbled and then plopped down in her dad's old recliner, sending a fury of allergens up around him. He sneezed and coughed until he dropped his head to his hands and rubbed his temples.

"What's wrong?" Trace asked. She grabbed one of the boxes Kat had sent over and began to clear off the coffee table of her father's *Popular Mechanics* and *Boat* magazines. An ashtray she'd made him when she was seven, despite no one smoking in the house, sat like a time portal to a past life she didn't want to visit. With a shallow breath, she picked up the glossy, jagged, over-painted ceramic and eyed the loose change inside.

"Put the stuff to keep in the box and toss the rest into the corner and I'll take it to the dump."

"The dump?" Trace slammed the box down on the table with a thump. "You make it sound like my father's things can be discarded like they were all junk." She snatched a half-ripped magazine from the box and held it up at him. "What if this is important? What if I want to keep it because I like to relax with a good magazine?"

"You going to read that later, are you?" Dustin lifted his head and a brow at her. Not just any brow. The one with the tiny scar that she imagined he'd gotten in a bar fight, but in reality he'd probably sustained the injury from a woman smacking him with her purse.

"Yeah, why not. I love skimming through classic magazines." Trace pushed her shoulders back. "So what?"

"I didn't know you enjoyed looking at naked women…"

"What?" She held the paper away from her as far as her

arms could reach. Perhaps due to her nearly fifty-year-old eyes not being able to read too close, or maybe because she couldn't believe her father had such smut in his house. She dropped it like a spiny urchin with flaming spikes.

Dustin laughed.

She hated being laughed at. She'd been laughed at plenty growing up. Now that she was older, she didn't have to take it. "Forget it. I'll do this myself."

He resumed rubbing his temples. "I knew you didn't have a sense of humor. The first day we met, I knew you were a bitter woman."

"Was that before or after you tripped over yourself at the sight of me at Friendship Beach?" She lifted her chin proud and high.

He didn't answer, which aggravated her. Instead, he rubbed his temples more.

"What's wrong with you?"

"Nothing. Headache is all. Had it for days now." His eyes remained closed, and she knew they'd never get any work done if he didn't feel better. "I told you to leave. I've got this."

"Obviously you don't." He pointed at the magazine with one hand while the other one continued to assault his temple with man hands that would push through his skull in a minute.

Trace eyed Dustin suspiciously, but he did look flushed. "You have any other symptoms? Is your urine dark?"

He dropped both hands to his knees. "You say the strangest things." He bolted up from the chair but smacked the ground hard on his knees.

"Lightheaded by chance?" She retrieved a bottle of water with electrolytes from her cooler and handed it to him. "Here, drink this. You're suffering from dehydration. You haven't been drinking enough water."

He squinted up at her and opened his mouth as if to argue but then took the water bottle from her and unscrewed the cap. "Thanks."

"What?" She blinked at him, unsure she'd heard the high and mighty Dustin say something other than self-praise. "I mean, you're welcome. Rest. I'll get to work." She tossed a few magazines into a pile near the opened front door, and the rest filled up a quarter of the box.

"I'll be fine in a minute. I said I'd help." He pushed up but only far enough to slide his butt into the chair. "Perhaps in a few minutes."

"It's fine." Trace moved to the shelf on the wall that separated the main room from the kitchen and dusted a few conch shells that she and her father had brought home for dinner one night when she was around ten. She'd insisted on keeping the beautiful shells to decorate their home. He'd agreed. Of course, Dad had always agreed with everything she'd wanted.

"Looks like your father had a regular bachelor pad. Did your parents divorce when you were young?"

"No, my mother died. My father never remarried. He raised me and said I was the only thing he ever needed in his life."

Dustin took a long sip of his drink. "I'm sorry. It must've been tough growing up without a mother."

"Yes and no." Trace picked up a picture of her, her dad, and all her friends at a beach picnic on a remote sand bar. "My father gave me the best life. An original childhood. Sure, I didn't have much, but we were happy. I climbed trees, slept in the woods, swam with sharks and dolphins."

"That's a good life?" Dustin asked in a you're-insane tone.

"Sharks aren't meant to be pets or playmates. You know that, right?"

"They're harmless." She streaked her finger across the pane, smearing the dust so she could see the picture more clearly. Her father was tall, handsome, dark-skinned from the sun, and kept his hair shaggy and long. A true beach bum with a heart. "I loved the freedom he allowed me. There was no curfew or rules, only respect and honesty."

Dustin blew out a long breath and ran a hand through his dark, sweat-drenched curly hair in that James Bond exiting an ocean kind of way he'd perfected. But he wasn't putting on a show or strutting around to be noticed at the moment. "Sounds like paradise. My family was nothing like that."

"How were they?" She placed the picture frame in a box and rubbed at a stain on the edge of the old conch shell.

"Rules, regulations, reputation," Dustin said in a commanding officer tone.

"That sounds cold and distant." Trace set the conch shell into the box and eyed Dustin's red face. He looked miserable, but she wasn't sure if it was from the heat, dehydration, or his family.

"Cold and calculating is what my ex-girlfriend called me. And she wasn't the first and probably not the last. That stuck with me."

"Why's that?"

"Because it was true. For as many years as I'd fought becoming my parents, I realized I was their clone. They were proud of me."

"Were? I'm so sorry. I didn't know you'd lost your parents too." A paper cut–sized opening made her feel a loose connection to the man sitting broken in front of her. She couldn't allow herself to feel something for a man like this, so she averted her gaze to the old television that still had turn dials. Her father had never thrown anything out unless it was beyond repair.

"They're still alive and living in a mansion with servants. A nurse comes by to handle medicines for my father since his stroke, but they're relatively healthy." Dustin downed the rest of the beverage. "I say were because when I sold my company and moved here, they told me I was having a midlife crisis and that I shouldn't come around until I came to my senses."

"Are you?" She dared another glance and found him suffering still. That thin laceration grew into a razor slice, allowing her to feel enough to want to help him, so she grabbed her neck gator, poured cold water from the cooler over it, and held it out to him. When he blinked at her as if she were handing him a barracuda, she placed it on the back of his neck. "Here. It'll help keep you cool."

"Thanks. And no."

"No?"

"I'm not having a midlife crisis. I'm having a midlife real-ization. Realization that life is too short to be so worried about money and success. It's time to live my life, and when Trevor begged me to buy the hotel and I saw how happy he was here... Well, I decided to jump into the deep end of happily ever after before I realized I could drown."

"You can't swim?" Trace eyed the ocean through the window.

"Don't get any ideas."

"You're going to have to go swimming with me," Trace said and meant it. She couldn't imagine anyone not experiencing life underwater. He didn't know what he was missing. "How are you going to run an oceanfront hotel and not know how to swim?"

He pinched the bridge of his nose. "Not happening, so move on. Besides, we have too much work to do to go swimming."

Trace collapsed on the ottoman by his side. "So you're not scared of sharks? You just used that as an excuse?" That razor slit in her resolve broke open into a gaping wound, so she shooed his hand away from his nose and stood behind him.

He tensed and eyed her over his shoulder. "Oh, no. I'm scared of sharks. And I didn't say that I couldn't swim. You said that."

She turned his head to face forward and tugged his back to the chair.

"What are you doing?" His shoulders were stiff, neck straight and rigid.

"Fixing you so we can get to work and I can get you into the ocean." With small, soothing rotations, she smoothed the wrinkles from his forehead.

"You can't. It won't work. I get these headaches all the time. It's stress."

"So stop stressing." She ran her palm down over his eyes so he'd close them, and she massaged his face and rubbed his earlobes. His soft skin over his chiseled features was not lost on her, but she ignored the way a connection sparked between her fingertips and his body. "If I can tame lions and alligators, I can tame you.

"Many women have tried, hon."

"Blah. Stop talking. Better yet, get over yourself already and be quiet. All you do is boast or lie. You'd be handsome if you didn't speak."

"I knew you liked me." He stilled, stretched his legs out in front of him, and dropped his head back. "Ohhhh. Ummmm. That's nice."

"I'm not the one who liked you. You liked me. Trevor told Jewels your eyes popped from your head when you saw me in a dress. Hope you took a picture because that's never happening again."

Dustin stilled her hand and looked up at her. His firm lips didn't pull into that wicked grin of his, nor did his dark lashes flutter in that flirtatious way he had. Instead, his eyes softened and he said, "You're right. I did notice you."

She didn't know what to say, but she knew the compliment was only meant to distract her. That was Dustin's way. To distract and then attack. She swiveled his head forward and returned to massaging the back of his neck.

"You go to massage therapy school?" he asked, his tone clearly saying they'd forget what he'd said and move on.

"No. I learned the trick working with dogs on a television show. They called me in to assess the movie set for animal abuse, and I figured out that the lights and sounds were stressing the animals out. I would rub their face and ears at certain trigger points to relax them. They were able to work again and not be upset."

"You're comparing me to some mutts?"

"If the paw fits."

"What other men have you tried this on to get what you want?" Dustin sighed, and his arms fell to the sides of the chair. "Just to warn you, I'm immune to women's charms, including yours. You won't change me."

"Rowan." Trace slid her fingers down to his shirt collar and pushed her thumbs to the pressure points along his shoulders and then along his cervical spine.

"Seriously? Rowan? What kind of name is that? He even sounds like a player."

Trace fought not to giggle. "Oh, he was. Tall, lean yet

muscular, powerful. I mean, when Rowan strutted into a room, everyone stopped what they were doing. He was that memorable." She stopped rubbing his neck and flicked him in the ear. "Now, let's get to work so we can go for that swim."

"So is that the man who made you hate all handsome, self-assured good guys?" Dustin stood. He looked better—less red and more relaxed.

"Not hate. Just 'cause I'm not attracted to a man or don't want to deal with his overactive self-worth doesn't mean I dislike all men. But, yes, Rowan did ruin all others for me. I mean, no man I've ever met since has lived up to my expectations after Rowan. He was so memorable and large and solid."

"Okay, enough. I get it." Dustin grabbed a box and swiped a shelf full of old junk into the cardboard container.

Trace enjoyed stabbing at Dustin's ego. "What's wrong? Jealous?"

"Me? Of a man? Never." Dustin set the box down on the coffee table and eyed the side table.

"You know, he wasn't much different than you, though."

"Really?" Dustin's voice hitched with a sense of pride.

"Yeah, he would relax when I tried to massage the tension away. He'd fall asleep when I rubbed his long, lean belly."

"Belly? Wait a second. Are you talking about a dog again?" Dustin put his hands on his hips in that wide, commanding stance of his.

"No." Trace couldn't believe they'd gone from shooting hateful remarks to fun banter, but she liked this better. Perhaps because she was the one winning this time. And he wasn't manipulating her to get what he wanted. "He's eight feet. Ever met a dog eight feet long?"

Dustin crossed his arms over his large chest and looked down at her. "No human is eight feet tall."

"Oh, there are, but Rowan wasn't a human. He was a gator."

"Well, I can't compete with that." To her surprise, he didn't get angry at her for teasing him. He laughed. A sincere, easygoing sound that made Trace believe he might actually be a decent person after all.

Almost.

CHAPTER TWELVE

DUSTIN SEALED the twelfth box and stacked it on top of the others near the door. His headache had diminished to a dull roar, despite the shirt-clinging, sweat-slicked, corrosive environment of sun, sand, and sauna steam.

He watched a proud Trace working to near exhaustion. The woman had two speeds: fast and exhaustive. But how did a woman in shorts, worn T-shirt, and hair pulled back look good cleaning a home?

A flickering of happiness knocked at him. When was the last time he was happy?

Perhaps Trevor was right. He did overcompensate for her rejection by lashing out. But how was he supposed to handle a woman who wasn't interested in him? He hadn't had to deal with that since fifth grade when a girl pushed him off a swing when he tried to kiss her. Maybe Trevor was right and she was attracted to him to, but not his—what did Trevor call it again? Oh, right, cocky character.

Trace stood, staring at a book she'd moved around the room several times. Trevor was right. She wasn't the usual

CIARA KNIGHT

kind of woman Dustin went for. She was all wrong for him and it would never work, but he could tone down his flirtations enough to be friends. And right now, with the way she studied the book in her hand and her delicious, off-limit lips drooped into a frown, she needed a friend, not a hook-up. "We could take a break."

Trace set the book down once more. "We had a break."

"That was two hours ago and a pound of fluid secreted from my pores."

"Dramatic much?" She tilted her head. Her blonde hair pulled up in a ponytail made her neck look as long as Audrey Hepburn's. He'd loved those old movies he'd watched with his grandmother for their special days when he'd escaped his parents' suffocating house.

He didn't answer. Instead, he watched her and processed what he saw instead of lunging into some teasing comments like a child with a schoolyard crush.

When she'd packed the first box, she'd held the book above the rest of the stuff but set it on the couch before she sealed the box and went to box two. That time, she set it in the box but took it back out and set it on the shelf. "What's the book?"

She shrugged. "Nothing really."

"It has to be something. You keep holding on to it." He picked up the side table and set it by the door, careful not to break the rotting wood. Despite everything in this rotted old shack being unsalvageable, he'd realized how much she struggled to let any of it go. He couldn't claim to understand, but if he ever wanted to make things work, he needed to respect her struggle.

"It's not because of what the book is. It's that I can't figure out why my father left it for me."

Dustin joined her by the desk near the hallway and looked

90

over her shoulder—which wasn't tough to do since she was five-foot-nothing. The book was old and worn, *Anne of Green Gables*. He'd heard of the movie before from a woman he dated but didn't know it was a book. "It looks old."

She touched the cracked edges as if to read a hidden message telepathically. "Had it since I was in middle school, I think."

"What's significant about it?"

"I guess I can't pack it because I can't understand why my father left it wrapped for me."

"Did he used to read it to you?" Dustin asked, hoping to help her process whatever she needed to so they could be done for the day.

"No, not that I remember. I haven't seen it in over thirty years, though." Trace's voice dipped eight feet below ground.

Dustin understood the parent struggle. "I'm estranged from my mother and father right now too. I dread going home and have avoided it at all costs in recent years."

"No."

"No?" he asked, but when she looked up with misty eyes he knew she raged an internal war with her past.

"We weren't estranged. I never realized it, but he'd always meet me out somewhere or come visit me at Jewels's the two times I came home. We met in Jamaica once when I convinced him to fly out to go on a fishing trip with me, but other than that, we didn't see much of each other." She shrugged. "Not that I didn't want to. I was just always busy, and he never encouraged me to come home. It was as if he didn't want me to. We were so close growing up. He was my everything. I guess it kind of hurt my feelings, believing he'd moved on with his life and didn't have room for me. As if he'd only pretended that he wanted me around all those years." She turned and eyed the four corners of the room. "But obviously he hadn't moved on."

"That infamous Summer Island phone line didn't send you word about him on occasion?" Dustin asked, recalling Trevor's mention of how everyone in town knew everything and they didn't even need to text.

"The Salty Breeze Gossip Line only said he'd become a hermit. But that was Dad. He liked to be alone and free." She hopped up on the desk and held on to the memory. "When I was twelve, I was a handful. I'm surprised my father put up with me. I was angry at the world."

"Sounds like most twelve-year-olds."

She chuckled. "Based on my torturous, short-lived stint volunteering at the San Diego Zoo to teach children about sea life, I'd agree. But I was worse."

He settled in next to her, their arms touching. It was too hot to sit that close to anyone, but he didn't mind. He liked this side of Trace. The vulnerability and openness. There was something about her, an honesty he'd never witnessed in a woman before. It was refreshing. Even if too dramatic at times. "In what way?"

"In all ways." She dropped her hands, still clutching the book in her lap. "I was mad over stupid things like clothes and money."

"But you said you had a great life." He shouldered her, sending her swaying away from him, which made him regret his movement until she returned to him skin-to-skin.

"Yes, the living part, the freedom, that was all fantastic. The teasing, not so much. Kids are cruel. They'd chant 'little tomboy' at me on my way to school. Rhonda even posted a picture of me in the girls' locker room in high school with the caption *HELP THE NEEDY.* The kids knew I couldn't afford my own clothes or the latest music or a car or anything. It made life difficult once I reached middle school. My father tried. He worked two jobs and anything odd on the weekends he could manage. But I was ungrateful for his sacrifice. All I cared about was what those kids thought of me."

The way her head fell, chin to chest, made him want to pull her in for a hug to comfort her. She looked lost, confused, upset. Had he done that to her by trying to demolish her childhood home? "I'm sorry. Rhonda told me that this place meant nothing to you, and I listened. I shouldn't have. I never meant to tear down something so important to you. I'm not heartless."

She shot straight and slid him a sideways glower that said she didn't need anyone. "It doesn't." She tossed the book into the box and headed to the kitchen. "It did to him, though."

That's when he knew the truth. Trace didn't want to face something in this house. He wasn't sure what memory she hid away from, but he didn't like how it made her switch back to her distant, angry voice and posture.

When the sun set below the trees, he decided enough was enough. "Without electricity, we need to stop."

"Why? We can get some lanterns or candles." She dropped a box of pots and pans next to the pile that nearly reached the ceiling.

"Are you a camel?"

She blinked at him. "What?"

"I figured you spoke animal, so I was trying to relate. I'm asking if you can go days without eating, because I can't."

"First of all, you don't speak animal. Trust me. Secondly, camels don't need water."

"Actually, they can last months without food, too." Dustin

said, pride bubbling to the surface for one-upping her on animal speak.

Trace snagged her phone off the Formica counter and plugged away with her thumbs. "Hmmm, you're right. I'm afraid I'm not up on my land creatures. How'd you know that?"

His pride whirled around the drain of embarrassment. "That's not important."

The buzzing around his head gave him a way out of the conversation, and he took it at a full sprint. "Bugs are closing in." He pointed to the open door. "And it's too hot to shut that. I'll buy you dinner if you'll agree to call it quits for today."

"Avoid much?" She didn't stop working, so he turned up the heat.

"Listen, I just thought you might like a nice evening out. I'll take you to a fancy restaurant, and we can have drinks and…"

"And what? Does that work on the ladies? Offering to spend money on them so you can get what you want? News flash, not interested. I've been poor my entire life, and I won't fall for some money being thrown around to impress me into your bed."

"That's not what I was doing. If it was, you'd be interested. Trust me." Dustin grabbed his wallet and keys.

"Seriously? I wounded your pride so you're going to run away? Are you really that insecure, or are you scared of me?" Trace squatted and reorganized the box he'd only finished packing a few minutes ago. "Don't feel bad. Most men aren't strong enough to handle me. I'm used to it."

"I don't run. And I'm not scared of you. I can handle any woman. I've had plenty of practice. My ego can take what you throw at it, especially when you're only avoiding your true attraction for me." Dustin chuckled to make sure she knew he was only teasing. "Besides, I know exactly who you are, and nothing you do could be more than I can handle."

She shoved the box toward him and stood, facing him with a smile like one of those women on her dad's *Playboy* magazines. With a hip sway that would make Kim Kardashian look like a paper doll, she sashayed toward him. "You're right. We should take a break. I'll go shower," she said in a seductive you-could-join-me tone... or so his man-gination told him. "Then I'll do my hair and make-up. I'll put on a nice, hip-hugging dress." She pressed one finger to her plump lips. "Would that work?"

"Yes—I mean no." He took a step back, his thighs hitting the desk. Mayday alerts sounding in his head. "Ah, sure."

She laughed, a full-on girly laugh.

"What's so funny?"

"You and your 'I know everything about everyone' way." Trace snapped to her rigid frame with her shoulders pushed back. "To think you'd believe I'd put on a dress for you. I won't put on a dress for any man. Especially not you."

CHAPTER THIRTEEN

TRACE SHUFFLED through the woods side-by-side with Dustin in silence. Perhaps she'd been too hard on him.

The way he'd listened to her and asked questions about her past made her think he actually cared about her and not just the hotel and business. But Robert Remming had seemed overly interested in everything about her, and it had only been an act.

No way she'd be manipulated by a fancy meal and wooing again.

They reached the hotel, and she paused at the edge of the docks, looking up the small hill toward the hotel and Trevor's place. "Dutch. Not a date." She continued ahead, assuming that was the end of the conversation, but he followed by her side.

"Non-date, but I pay." He thrust out his hand like a business deal.

"Why would you pay? You just worked on my father's house for hours with me pushing you to do something you hate for someone you don't like." Trace huffed, wishing she could read people better. If she had Wind's gift for that, she would've known Robert had been playing her like a teenager on a hoverboard.

Most people were a mystery to her, and with Dustin—despite their easy banter and obvious physical attraction—she didn't know the right thing to say or do.

"Is that what you think?" Dustin trotted ahead, then turned in a football field block position.

She stopped short of the tackle, but the way he looked at her caused a sensual shiver through her body. His gaze was intense, searching—for what, she didn't know, but she couldn't hold it, so she looked toward the one thing in the world that was always there… The ocean.

"I know your type, and I'm nothing more than a sand flea at your barbeque. If you could, you'd swat me away."

Hands. Strong hands. Hands that sent a heat up her shoulders, over her neck, and down her spine. Hands that promised peace, hope, security wrapped around her biceps and squeezed. Squeezed the breath from her lungs. She blinked at him and told herself, *They are just hands. Hands that lie.*

"Let me tell you something, young lady." Dustin's gaze narrowed. His chin set, brow furrowed. But then he took in a breath and dropped his head, still holding her like a life preserver in a storm. "No. You're right. That is the type of man I am…or was."

His voice, the tone sharp and pained, slapped her with realization. The man struggled, but with what? "Was?" she asked, her voice soft and probing.

"I hope it's how I was and not who I'll be."

He released his grasp and took a step back. She thought she'd drown from the loss of his unexpected, unrequested, unnerving touch. A touch she hadn't asked for or wanted but needed. For the first time in years, her gut didn't feel like she was stuck on a ship in a Category 5 hurricane surrounded by waterspouts. She shook off her crazy thoughts and watched the man look to her ocean as if he wanted to find something beyond his fear.

"I'm like the moon. Old, worn, and solid in where and who I am in this universe. But I don't want to be the moon. I've been the moon for too long, and all that resides on my planet is dust and craters."

"You're full of holes?" Trace tried to decipher his analogy, but she couldn't. Where were Jewels or Wind or Kat when she needed them?

"Yes. No. I mean..." He spun on his heels in the thatches of St. Augustine grass sprouting between dirt piles, but he didn't speak. He only looked to her as if she was supposed to say what he couldn't.

"I'm sorry. I don't speak man. Heck, I've been accused by more than one ex-boyfriend that I don't speak human. Not that you're my... What I mean is..."

He laughed. "How could you decipher what I can't even figure out? I'm rambling. All I mean to say is that I came to Summer Island to find something Trevor discovered, but according to him I can't find something if I'm not willing to look."

"What are you looking for?" Trace asked, wishing he'd spit out what he really meant.

"I don't know." Dustin moved in. His tall frame and wide shoulders reminded her of a Navy SEAL she'd known when she'd been working on a top-secret research project in the middle of the Indian Ocean. Yet, his soft dark curls, which had grown since he'd arrived, framed a handsome, less angular face.

Trace looked at her tennis shoes. This was the moment when she usually ran from a conversation. When she didn't have answers or understand what someone was talking about.

Dustin snagged her fingers with a light touch. "But you could help me figure it out. Dinner?"

Trace thought about awkward conversations discussing moons and the uncomfortable mention of feelings and all other subjects that she hated to talk about. Maybe her friends were right and she was emotionally stunted at birth or what Rhonda told everyone about her being raised by an animal so she didn't relate to humans. No, this was a bad idea. They needed to work together and get the job done. That's what Trace did best. No entanglements. Only work. And she'd never, ever allow another Robert into her heart. "Yes."

"Yes?" Dustin lit up like a full moon.

Wait, was that all he needed? A little light in his life? Dang, no, this was impossible, she had no gift at reading people.

"I don't know if I can help with figuring out why you're a rock in the sky, so don't expect too much from me."

"No worries. I won't try to compare myself with an inanimate object again. Casual conversation, non-date, good food, and I pay." Dustin held out his hand once more.

"Limited conversation, non-date, okay food, and Dutch." She took his hand.

He held it tight and leaned in. "Limited conversation, non-date, average food, and I'm paying." He shook and then released her hand and strutted up the hill with that I-bested-you swagger.

"You didn't win that. It was a compromise," she shouted before tromping through the weeds and sand.

"A compromise with you is a win," he shouted.

Trace marched up the street, chastising herself for being

caught up in the Devilish Dustin Drama, and bolted through the front door of Jewels's house to avoid Win and Jewels. She showered, all the time having a mental argument about why she'd said yes to the all-wrong-for-her man. She returned to the guest room to find Houdini with a knowing glance, staring at her suitcase as if to say, *if I could speak, I'd tell them about that letter.* He reached out with his paw and set it on a dress. He seemed to say, *Ha-ha. This is payback for hiding the truth.*

Wind, ex-best friend turned traitor, bounced like a cartoon character on two-pounds of Skittles. "Wear this," she said in an obnoxious unicorn and rainbows fantasy tone.

"It's a dress." Trace snatched a pair of shorts, T-shirt, and a sports bra from her duffel. "Why would I wear that?"

"Date with Dustin," Wind announced.

"Not a date. You're the one who's dating him." Trace's chest tightened. Her breath caught between a way out and an off-ramp she didn't want to take.

"Dustin and I are too similar, and opposites attract. And you two are definitely opposites." She held up the dress, but Trace tightened the towel around her body as if it would serve as her shield.

Houdini chattered in ferret peer pressure.

Trace shook her head at him. "Not you, too."

Wind pouted with a lip that looked like a filler injection had gone rogue. "Come on. It's a date with Dustin. Trust me, this is soooo much better."

"What are you? Twelve?" Trace faced the wall and put on her sports bra and T-shirt.

"Modest. Geesh. Not like we didn't all jump in the ocean naked as kids."

"That was so when we skipped classes to go swimming

and we didn't have any other clothes to wear, we could return to school without getting caught."

"Still, I thought at our age, modesty was a misnomer."

"At our age, modesty is a must. Especially when my spare tire has deflated from age."

Wind shot up and turned her around, lifting her shirt and poking a finger in her belly button, the one sensitive spot she hated anyone to touch. It was like someone stuck a finger inside her and touched her light socket, zapping her insides. "Stop that."

"Still don't like it?" Wind dropped her shirt and picked up the dress from the bed. "Please, you're in better shape than any of us. You've still got long, lean muscles from swimming. And how'd you avoid sun damage in your profession? Wait, you had to have that lasered off."

"Right, the woman who has slept in tents and bunkrooms with twenty other people to avoid paying for a hotel has money to blow on skin treatments."

"Compromise?" Wind leaned out the door and waved. "Do you own a real bra?"

Trace huffed. "Yes, of course."

Jewels joined them, holding her own clothes. "Wear these capri pants. Dress isn't you. Shorts aren't good for dinner with mosquitoes and are too casual."

Trace plopped down on the bed. Her mind was spinning with questions, as if she was fifteen again. Why'd she care what Dustin said or wanted? He had been her enemy. "Why would someone think they were a moon?"

Jewels placed the outfit on her lap and picked up Houdini, who now purred louder than a 1950s marine engine. "What do you mean?"

Trace threw her hands up. "I don't know. I mean, Dustin

said he was like a moon. You know I don't like to read between the lines."

Wind sat on the bed by her other side, leaving Trace as the meat in the friendship sandwich. She folded the dress, as if surrendering to the idea of putting Trace into it. "It means he's alone, far away, and cold. In other words, he's lonely and lost and looking for the sun."

Trace shot up straight. "You got all that? Are you like a man whisperer or something?"

"Me? Yes." Wind smiled in her theatrical way, so Trace braced for a performance, but she didn't give one. Instead, Wind patted Trace's leg. "Don't worry. You'll figure it out. I honestly think you and Dustin are perfect for each other. Neither of you know it yet."

"Do you really trust the man? I mean, he's like... others."

Jewels and Wind shot a knowing look to each other, and then their arms both landed around her shoulders. "Not every man is the same."

Wind played with the back of her hair, relaxing her into compliance. "Dustin's a good man. Yes, you can trust him."

Trust him? Did it mean anything that her friends judged him trustworthy?

"Trace, are you ever going to tell us what happened?"

Trace bolted from their embrace. "Nothing to tell." She raced to the bathroom, her heart, pulse, and breath rapid and erratic. She shut the door and fell against it, huffing and puffing. She needed to escape the idea of her and Dustin. They might understand men, but they didn't understand how low and dirty they could be.

No. No. No. She'd never trust another man again.

CHAPTER FOURTEEN

DUSTIN HELD up his long-sleeved dress shirt and knew it would be drenched in sweat by the time he reached the car in the scorching Florida heat. Too hot, too uncomfortable, and too wrong for going out with Trace on a non-date. "Hey, Trevor. You got one of those short-sleeved shirts I could borrow?"

"You mean the ones that you make fun of, calling me a Shriveling Salty Senior?" Trevor hollered up from the downstairs living room.

Dustin stepped out of his eight-by-eight claustrophobic closet-sized room and looked over the balcony at Trevor with his feet up on the coffee table and computer in his lap. "Yeah, but that's you in your old-man bod. I'll rock the look. Besides. It's hotter than a skillet set on the sun."

"You keep telling yourself that, but desperation doesn't look distinguished on you." Trevor set the computer on the coffee table and climbed the steps to the second floor. "If you want to dress to impress Trace, then I've got the perfect outfit for you."

"I didn't ask for a makeover. I'm not a thirteen-year-old girl. A shirt, dude. That's all I wanted. I've ordered some clothes, but they haven't arrived. Apparently even the Zon can't deliver in a day out here."

Trevor disappeared into his closet and came out holding a linen shirt with a lavender stripe down the front.

Dustin shot his arms up in front of him in a barrier to bad fashion. "No. Not happening. I'm not wearing that. Give me the plain white one."

"It's dirty."

Dustin eyed the hamper. "How dirty?"

Trevor removed the frou-frou shirt from the hanger, balled it up, and threw it at him. "This is Florida. The shirt smelled five minutes after I put it on. Take this or don't and wear one of your stiff-neck, suffocating shirts."

Dustin snarled. "First you drag me out here, and now you force me to dress in this girl shirt."

"There's a statute of limitations on you blaming me for your decision to move here. And that's not a girl's shirt." He shoved his pointer finger into Dustin's chest. "Besides, you won't fit in anything I own."

"You calling me fat?"

"If the shirt fits." Trevor laughed and buddy-slapped Dustin's shoulder on his way to the hallway. "I'm talking about your muscles. You've always been the muscle-strutting type. Don't deny it."

"Can't help it if I look good." Dustin slid the sleeves of the linen sissy shirt over his shoulders and buttoned it. Much cooler than his dress clothes but not a grimy work T-shirt. It'd have to do, light purple stripe and all. "Wait, why do you own this shirt? It's a large. You're at best a medium."

"Wind sent it over this morning. She bet you'd have a date

with Trace by this afternoon. You owe me twenty bucks by the way." Trevor's voice faded with each step he took down to the living room.

Dustin grunted, grabbed his wallet and keys. "Non-date. Both of us have to eat, and I'm sick of eating with your ugly manipulating mug," he shouted over the balcony.

Trevor held a hand to his heart. "I'm hurt."

"Keep on and you will be." He shuffled down the steps to the main floor. "I was going to offer to bring you something home, but forget it. You can starve."

"Got a hot date of my own, so no worries. Jewels and I are going for a moonlight picnic on a sandbar," Trevor said, sounding like he'd lose his bachelor status at any moment. Ugh. Too soon. Way too soon to be chained to another woman since it hadn't been that long since Marsha had dumped him like a rabid raccoon. Jewels was nice and all, but who wanted to rush from one marriage to the next? Dustin had managed to avoid it his entire life. Didn't get why anyone wanted to be part of that institution.

He drove the two blocks to Jewels's house. Wind's car was out front. With one hand on the door handle, he hesitated. The shirt. Had Wind sent it as a joke and he was about to deliver the punchline to the front door? He'd deserve it. Not sure why, but when it came to women, he'd realized a long time ago that he provoked their anger and resentment. He had to, or it wouldn't have happened so often.

With a deep breath, he wrenched the car door open and marched up the front walk.

Wind opened the door before he reached the front step. A coldness whispered up his spine. "Good evening, handsome. Ready for your big date?"

"Um… non-date." He shifted between his feet and ran a hand through his hair. "Listen, I hope you don't think—"

"That you will break Trace's heart?" Wind sauntered to the last step, placed a hand on his shoulder, and leaned in as if to kiss him. "Listen, relax. I'm not upset. I'd hoped you'd ask her out. But if you hurt her…" She tapped his lips with a finger from her free hand. "Well, you won't have to worry about swimming with sharks, because I'll feed you to a gator."

Wind pirouetted and opened the front door, waving him inside.

Houdini scurried into the room, up the gangway, around the platform, and hopped onto his shoulder, chattering as if giving him the big brother speech.

"You tell him, Houdini." Wind pointed to the melodramatic ferret he was sure she had sent to acting school. He reached up to pet him, but Houdini smacked his hand away, hopped over the couch, and then disappeared down the hallway.

"You remember what I said." She mimed a knife across her throat, hanging, and stabbing.

Dustin smiled, grinning away her threat. He wrapped his arm around her shoulders and pulled her into his side. "No worries. We're not dating. Complete opposites don't even begin to define us as a couple."

Wind broke free of him, laughing with Broadway projection.

"What's so funny?" he grumbled.

"You." She fanned her face. "In your denial, you admitted you liked her."

"What? No I didn't." Did he? Wait, no. He didn't think of her as more than a friend. A sexy, passionate, beautiful friend. But a friend. "How'd I do that?"

"You said couple, which means you've thought about it. Besides, you protest more when you are tiptoeing around something."

"How would you know that?" Dustin lowered his voice to a conciliatory whisper.

"Because unlike Trace, who deserves better than either of our shallow selves, we are too much alike." Wind winked and whirled to face the hallway. "Trace, your date's here."

"Non-date," she shouted from an open door on the right. Trace marched to the edge of the hall in a blue button-up shirt that highlighted her waist, her breasts, her eyes.

"What?" Trace stared down at her feet and then back at him. "You'd think I was wearing a dress."

Wind shoved a handbag at her. "Pepper spray in here in case he gets handsy."

He hoped she was kidding.

Based on Trace's grimace, she didn't want to carry it, but then she huffed and pulled a wad of money and cards from her pocket and shoved it into the purse. "Let's go."

He rushed to the door to open it for her, but he wasn't fast enough and his hand covered hers on the knob. If he wasn't wrong, she gasped at his touch.

She took in a deep breath, calling his attention to her chest. Her gaze snapped to him with a glower. "Non-date. Remember?" She tugged her shirt around her neck and wrenched the door open. "By the way, nice shirt. Wind dress you?"

She marched outside, leaving Dustin to look to Wind.

"Stop treating her like you would a normal date. She deserves better. She's not a filet on your plate. She's a flower in a vase at the center of the table."

"What's that supposed to mean?"

Wind fluttered away, leaving him to decipher her cryptic message. A problem even Pythagoras couldn't solve.

CHAPTER FIFTEEN

TRACE STOOD AT THE CAR, eyeing the tiny interior. She needed to keep her distance from Dustin and her wayward thoughts of a man oh so wrong for her. Darn friends. It was their fault. Wind and Jewels filled her head with garbage.

Dustin reached the end of the steps, and she panicked. "Let's walk." She took off, hands clasped in front of her, the bag swinging at her side.

"Wait. No. I was taking us to Cocoa Beach for dinner."

No, that would be a date. A romantic, remote restaurant with time for ideas. Bad ideas. Ideas that could lead her down the wrong path again. "Skip's is fine."

"You just want Skip to see me to tell Rhonda. I refuse to be a pawn in your war." He remained by the car.

"No, that's not it," she blurted but stopped walking.

"Then what is it?"

How could she explain to the man that she didn't trust herself in a car alone with him? She about-faced, marched to the car where Dustin waited holding the door open for her, and plopped into the passenger seat.

Dustin rounded the car, hopped in, and drove halfway to Cocoa Beach in silence. The sun drifted down, and Trace's thoughts slipped to her last day in Brazil before Matt had decided to impress her with thwarting the big oil rig. He'd been twenty years her junior, and she hadn't taken him seriously enough when he'd warned her the owner of the company was only using her to get what he wanted. How had someone so young understood so much? Her pulse revved, her heart revved, her sorrow revved to full throttle.

"Whatcha thinking about over there?" Dustin asked in a light tone, soothing her anxiety, or at least distracting her long enough so she could escape the memories.

"Nothing I can share with you."

He shot her a sideways glance and then pulled the car to a stop off the road onto the gravel shoulder.

"What are you doing?" Trace yanked at the constricting seat belt bruising her clavicle.

He gripped the steering wheel and didn't look at her. "Listen, I'd hoped to have a pleasant evening with you, but that isn't going to happen."

"I didn't mean..." She lifted her chin, fighting away the anxious tears she'd managed to escape when she'd seen Matt through the window, watching her embraced in a kiss with Robert Remming. Matt had tried to warn her about the man, but she hadn't listened. Maybe if she had, he wouldn't have rented a too-small boat in too-high seas to get proof of the oil rig's faulty procedures. A stunt that had cost him his life. "Take me home."

"No." He dropped his hands to his sides and leaned his head against the rest behind him. "Listen. I don't know how to do this. I've never been a direct man because I've never had to be. If you hate me for taking Rhonda's side, I understand, but I'm asking for another chance. A chance to work with you to fix up your father's place without resentment and hostility."

She blinked the tears away and forced the horrific memories from her mind. "I don't hate you."

Dustin released his seat belt and angled to face her. "Then what is it? Do I aggravate you that much? I know you think I'm shallow and that I'm a man who only cares about the next business deal—and maybe that was true once, but I came here to be a different person. I'll help any way I can with your father's place, and I vow never to try to tear it down again. I don't know how many times I have to say I'm sorry, but I didn't know at the time."

Trace fidgeted with her purse strap, trying to think of something to say. Honesty would be a good start, but was he really trying to change, or was it all an act like Robert? A game he'd play to get what he wanted. "I forgive you. Let's go eat." She channeled her inner Wind and produced an Emmy award-winning smile. "I'm hungry."

His head tilted to one side as if he needed to look at her from another angle. "So you trust me now?"

"Trust? I don't know that I trust anyone. Let's just try to work together without too many arguments." She could see in the way he returned to driving with his head a little lower and shoulders slumped that she hadn't given him what he wanted. She had no clue what that was. Wind's words filtered into her head. "Are you lonely?"

The car swerved. Dustin cleared his throat. "What?"

Trace didn't look at him. She kept her gaze on the passing trees and small homes. "You're the moon. A cold, lonely place where you're stranded far from any real contact with anyone."

Dustin laughed. Too loud for the small space of a car.

"Forget it." Trace twisted the strap of the purse into submission. "Last time I listen to Wind."

Dustin turned down a side road headed for the beach. "How does she do that? I mean, I thought I could read people in a boardroom. It's what's served me well in business. But Wind takes it to a new level. She can look at a person and know what they're thinking. You sure she isn't a mind reader instead of a dancer and actress?"

The tension in Trace's neck eased. "You have a point. The woman is gifted at knowing everything about everyone before they know it themselves. She told me that I'd go on a date with you before we went to the courthouse to fight it out. I told her she was crazy, but now look at us."

"On a date."

Trace snapped her gaze to Dustin, who drove with an ear-to-ear grin on his face. "Non-date."

"Oh no, that's not what you said. You said date." Dustin pulled into a parking lot and settled the car into a space before cutting the engine and looking at her. "If you insist. That means I pay." He bolted from the car before she could argue.

No. No. No. This wouldn't happen. She couldn't and wouldn't date another man like Robert. Not when a man like that cost a person too much.

Robert had cost Trace her job, her career, her dignity, her friend. Acid roiled and boiled up her throat. No, she couldn't trust Dustin. Not with her father's place, not with her future, not with her heart. She needed to be a moon. A dark, cold, lonely place where she couldn't be hurt or hurt anyone else.

The door flew open, and she pushed the emotions down, closed the compartment on loss and fear and hope. But when she stood up too fast and the emotions and lack of food took hold, dizzying her, Dustin was there to catch her. He held her up with his strong arms and made her believe he could be a man worth trusting.

Dustin wrapped one arm around her and brushed her hair from her face. "I've got you."

There were never three more terrorizing words Trace had ever heard in her life, because for the briefest of moments, she believed him.

CHAPTER SIXTEEN

THE RESTAURANT he'd carefully chosen so as not to be too fancy or romantic yet calm with a beautiful setting was anything but those things. Dustin kept his hand out to make sure some drunken college kid didn't bump into Trace.

He longed to ask her what she was thinking about, had been thinking about since they'd ridden over here together. It didn't look good. Something in her past, maybe? Part of him wanted to ask Wind about it, but that wouldn't be right. He couldn't go behind Trace's back to find out. If he'd gotten to know Trace at all, he knew one thing: She didn't like people who weren't honest.

"Why don't we go somewhere else?" he shouted over the bad karaoke echoing around the Tiki-style restaurant, pounding relentlessly against his head.

"Everything around here will be packed. It's summer and a weekend. We could go back to Skip's."

No. That wasn't happening. Dustin wanted a chance to get to know Trace better. He was intrigued and attracted to her, no matter how much he protested to everyone else. He eyed the bar area and spotted a takeout sign. The view out the back window was romantic with the moon setting, and it wasn't a windy evening. "I've got a better idea. Wait here."

He went to the sign and waited for a girl to return with bags for two other people. "How long to get an order to go?"

"Depends on what you want," she hollered over the music still blaring over the speaker.

"What's quick?"

"Special. Grilled grouper sandwich and fries are available now since the person just called and canceled their order."

"Sold." Dustin paid the lady and only hoped Trace liked the food. He knew she wasn't a vegetarian based on what she had eaten at Jewels's birthday party a few months back, so he took a shot, paid for the food, and joined Trace once more by the door. "Come on."

"What?" She cupped her ear, and he knew it was a losing battle to speak in this bar, so he took her by the hand and headed out the door. The fading of the ear-piercing music and the welcoming of the night air made him grasp the possibility that the night wasn't a complete loss.

Even better, he noticed at the edge of the beach, was that Trace hadn't pulled her hand away from his. Instead, she walked with their arms brushing on occasion. "I'm sorry about that place. I spent so much time looking for the best spot for a non-date with you that I never thought about what night of the week it was."

"You did?" Trace looked up at him with soft eyes. The anger and resentment had been replaced by an inquisitive raise of a brow.

"Yeah. I mean, I couldn't take you just anywhere, not after all that's happened between us so far. I wanted to take you for a nice meal to prove I wasn't a jerk who wanted to rip your childhood from you. The place couldn't be too fancy, or you'd accuse me of being full of myself and wanting to seduce you or something. I didn't want to take you to a dump because you deserve better. It couldn't be too romantic, or you'd think I was trying to trick you."

"Have I been that bad?" Trace chuckled. "Yeah, I guess I have. But in my defense, we didn't start off well."

Dustin paused halfway down the beach and hung a right, spotting a nice spot with smooth sand farther down the beach away from the music. "You weren't. It was justified. As a matter of fact, you impressed me. You showed your strength and were direct and firm. I'm an idiot. If you don't believe me, you can ask Trevor. He's told me that all the time since I arrived."

"Really? What else does Trevor tell you?" she asked.

Dustin stopped and set the bag down. His pulse double-timed. "I'm not sure how to answer that. If I tell you the truth, you might run. If I tell you a lie, you'll know it and hate me."

Trace tightened her grip on his hand. "Truth. I always want the truth, no matter what."

Dustin didn't look away, crack a joke, or throw out some compliment to win her affection. Instead, he did as she asked. "He told me that I should stop lying to myself and him because I was lost the day I saw you at Jewels's birthday party. You came out in that formfitting dress with more strength and drive and conviction and honesty and natural beauty than any woman I've ever met in my life."

The breeze picked up, sending Trace's hair flying like a halo around her head. He reached up and smoothed it away from her face while keeping hold of her with his other hand. He wanted to kiss her, pull her into his arms and show her how much he thought of her, but it was too soon.

"You see me that way? Not a cranky old lady who's always shouting about some tree-hugging cause?"

"Old, no. Cranky, sometimes. Tree hugger, often. Beautiful inside and out, always."

Trace looked up at him, and he thought he'd be lost forever in her gaze, but then she took a step away and his gut clenched tight. "Don't put me on a pedestal. I'm not that person. I'm not strong or brave or even good." Her voice cracked, and he couldn't imagine what Trace could have to be ashamed of in her life. The woman only cared about making things better.

He cupped her cheek. "I think you're exactly those things."

She shooed his hand away. "Don't. I'm not. I've done things. Things I don't want to talk about. Not with you, not with the girls, not with myself. I *can't* talk." She sank to the sand, pulled out the boxes of food, and plopped one on her lap.

He knelt by her side and scooted the box from her lap. "Is this about your father?" Dustin settled cross-legged in front of her and took both her hands.

"Not only my father." She looked to the stars, and he saw the tears pooling in her eyes. They were like acid on his heart. "It's more than that."

He stroked her hand with his thumb, willing her to trust him. "What is it?"

The surf crashed against the sand, drawing Trace's attention. She took in a stuttered breath and shook her head. "I-I caused a friend and his family great pain."

Seagulls squawked above, as if to question her words before he could. "I doubt that's possible."

The moon shone down on her skin, illuminating her face in a mystical glow, highlighting the pain etched in the lines around her eyes. "It's the truth. And what's worse is what I did to cause him so much pain. I was focused on myself. What I wanted and not on my job. He tried to show me the truth, and I didn't listen. So you see, Dustin Hawk, you have no reason to apologize to me for being a businessman who mows over people for what he wants. I'm worse. I pretend to be a good person, even though I'm not. I'm the kind of person that ruins people's lives or, worse, causes their deaths."

CHAPTER SEVENTEEN

TRACE THANKED the Lord for Dustin not pushing her for more information. He only held her and watched the moon and stars dazzle in the sky above. The night had gone from emotional to exceptional, but when he pulled up to the curb at Jewels's place, she didn't want the night to end. That scared her more than anything.

Dustin grasped the handle to the car door, but she stayed his movement with a soft touch to his forearm. "Wait."

He sat back and looked through the front windshield and then to her. "You don't need to tell me anything. But if you'd like to tell me what happened, I'll listen."

The tunnel at the edge of the fence jiggled, telling Trace that Houdini waited and watched. He was the perfect small-town, all-up-in-your-business resident.

She closed her eyes and knew that this was her way out of how she was feeling. The way her pulse quickened at the sight of Dustin. His touch heated her skin, and his kindness soothed her anger and resentment and hatred for herself. No. She didn't want to care for a man. Especially a man like

119

Dustin. Sure, he wasn't some important oil tycoon, but he was still a man of business and played the manipulation game. She'd witnessed his tactics firsthand. "I'm not allowed to talk about this, but I can't let you think I'm somebody I'm not. If you tell anyone, though—"

"I won't."

"I caused the death of my partner and friend while working to stop an oil rig from drilling off shore," she blurted at rib-stinging speed.

He covered her hand with his, but she pulled away. "No. Don't. I don't deserve your comfort. I've criticized all your manipulative ways, but I'm a hypocrite." She eyed the walk-away to Jewels's front door and the escape route from the truth. A truth she'd avoided for so long, she almost believed the lie that it wasn't her fault. She couldn't hold it in any longer. She had to tell someone, and if he hated her, it would be a solution to her attraction. And if he did tell someone, well, she deserved the punishment she'd receive for breaking the gag order.

Dustin didn't say anything, which drew her to look at him once more. The man only sat there with soft eyes. Not even a hint of judgment on his rugged and handsome face.

She took in a sweltering breath of denial and exhaled the facts. "I worked as the lead on a project to stop an oil company from damaging the ocean habitat. There were rumors that the company cut corners, causing even more impact on sea life. It was my job to fight them—a fight I was ready for—but then I was invited in to be part of the company instead of working against it." She fisted her hands. A sharp pain shot up her wrist.

Dustin reached over, unfurled her fingers, and entwined them with his.

She tugged to free herself. "No, I don't deserve your comfort."

He didn't let go. "I think you've been facing this alone long enough."

A dryness coated her tongue and throat. She thought she wouldn't be able to speak again, but she glanced out the front windshield at the sparkling, moonlit waves. "I'd been in the business so long, I thought I was immune to their tactics, and I was—the normal business bait and switch and guiding me toward what they wanted me to see. But then the head of the company flew me to the oil rig. Something that would never happen in US waters. He invited me for an unobstructed all-access tour of the rig, along with an inspector. That had never happened before. I'd always been a gnat on an ape, not worth anyone's attention. But there I was, getting the red carpet treatment."

Dustin shifted in his small seat and angled to face her as if there was nothing else in the world that meant more than her words.

She needed to get this out and stop paddling around the gapping whirlpool of regrets. "I was dazzled by the man. He convinced me that he had been thinking about getting out of the oil industry altogether. That he'd made his money and I'd changed his mind about what he was doing."

The tunnel at the edge of the walkway raddled again, as if her words were too much for Houdini to witness, not that he could hear from that distance or understand. If she could crawl into that tunnel with him at this moment, she would.

Say it. Confess and let him know the person you really are.

Trace cleared her throat. "I fell for him and his manipulation, hook, line, and drill. My intern and friend told me how I was being used, but I told him he was jealous. That he was my

121

intern and still had a lot to learn. I was a fool. And it cost him his life and my reputation."

Dustin tucked her hair behind her ear and tipped her chin to force her to look at him.

"I allowed myself to be used. And then I wouldn't listen. There I was, the one who thought no one ever listened to me, even though I knew I was in the right. I'd trained Matt. He only did something based on a story I'd told him about a stunt I pulled years ago." A coldness seeped out from her insides, and she shivered. "He looked up to me for so long. Had a crush on me, the way you do with teachers, so I dismissed him the way I'd been dismissed all those years."

Dustin didn't move, didn't blink, didn't breathe that Trace could hear. He only sat there, by her side, holding her hand and her grief. Finally he said, "I don't believe it was your fault."

"You don't know what happened."

"I don't have to. I know who you are, and you would never harm anyone."

"I was with the scoundrel Robert Remming, having wine and dinner and conversation and kissing when Matt took off on a boat too small for the waters, to unveil Robert's deception. If I hadn't been so caught up in being the center of attention in Robert's eyes, I would've been with Matt and he wouldn't have drowned trying to gather evidence. He was trapped beneath the small boat against the rig. A storm had rolled in, and he shouldn't have been out there. It's my fault the boy's dead."

The tears rolled down her cheeks. It was the first time she'd said the words aloud. Her gut churned and burned. Acid ate away at her insides.

Dustin released her and opened his door. She knew that

her past would open his eyes to who she was and why she didn't deserve any man in her life. With the back of her hand, she swiped away the tears, and then she grabbed her purse and opened the door. But when she stood to leave him and his ideal of her, he pulled her into him. His arms wrapped around her body like a shield against the pain.

The heat of him, the strength of him, soothed the battle inside. Her muscles relaxed, and her pulse slowed.

His lips pressed to her forehead, and he whispered, "It wasn't your fault."

But it was. If it hadn't been for her, Matt would be alive. And his parents wouldn't be mourning his death. A death she hadn't even answered their letters about.

Coward, that's what she was, and now she'd even dragged Dustin into her mess. A mess he could never speak about or she'd go to jail. Even if she could get around the gag order, Robert Remming claimed to have evidence linking her to Matt's death. It wouldn't matter if he'd made it up. He'd been right about one thing: The courts and world would believe his attorneys over a small-town activist.

Maybe that's why she'd told Dustin. She deserved prison. It had to be better than where she'd been living in purgatory.

CHAPTER EIGHTEEN

DUSTIN'S GUT CLENCHED TIGHT. A summer breeze cooled his anger for the man who had done this to Trace. He held the woman who curved perfectly into his body. Her wet cheek pressed to his chest and her tiny arms clinging around his middle melted him.

Trace's story convicted him. If he could change his past sins, he would, but he couldn't. He would face them, though. Trace had done nothing wrong and had nothing to be sorry for in her entire life. That man Robert Remming was at fault.

Dustin wanted to ask if the man had been arrested or if there was anything he could do, but he feared if he moved, spoke, breathed, she'd be gone. So he held her tight, wanting to make it better for her. "You can't blame yourself." He regretted speaking the moment she flinched.

She yanked free and looked up at him, dark eyelashes fluttering back tears.

He shook his head. "Don't shut me out. I'm not him. I'm not Robert." He didn't know if he said that to convince Trace or himself, but it didn't work either way. If he let her go now, he'd lose his chance with her. She'd never listen to him if she saw him as a Robert Remming.

The front door creaked, snapping Trace's attention. She bolted through the front iron gate, by an angry, cross-armed Wind, and out of sight. Out of his reach. He turned on his heels to retreat to his car. Emotions surged like floodwaters from a torrential downpour.

"Stop! No man's allowed to make Trace cry. What did you do?" She charged full-speed, with big hair, big nails, and big attitude. "It had to be bad to make the solid, dependable, fem-fighter cry."

Dustin knew he wouldn't escape Wind's assault without telling her something. "I didn't. Not directly." He eyed the walkway that led to Trace and thought about storming in there and making her see reason, but he knew that wouldn't work on her. This was her beastly battle with her past.

"What do you mean, not directly?" Wind huffed. One hand on her hip, the other one held as if to strike him.

"I can't say. It isn't my place." Dustin wrench open the car door. "Talk to her. She needs you."

Wind's lips relaxed from an I'm-going-to-kill-you line to an I-need-more-information frown. "What about you?"

Dustin crumbled into his car before his legs gave way. "What about me? I'm just here to fix up a hotel, sell it, and leave." He slammed the door and took off before he did something stupid. Like march into the house and confess to Trace that he cared about her in more than a business partner kind of way and that he wanted to make up for everything Robert Remming did to her until she believed in something again.

But he was the wrong man for that job. If anything, he'd let her down and make things worse for her. He was a selfish man. Ask any of his past girlfriends. He could never put Trace through another failed relationship with a man who didn't deserve her. No. Trace Latimer was better off without him.

He drove to Trevor's place. To his relief, Trevor wasn't home, so he pulled up Robert Remming on his cell phone and collapsed on the couch. The articles sang praise of a wealthy oil tycoon putting back his money into the environment. At the end of the third article, he spotted a picture of Trace working side by side on a beach cleaning up trash. The article created the image of a man helping a local activist for no other reason than to do his part.

Dustin knew the type. Heck, he'd taken the preschool class of how to manipulate in business, but this guy had graduated the master's program with honors. Dustin tossed his phone on the table with a thud and grunted loudly enough for his voice to echo around the empty house.

The front door flew open, and Trevor stormed into the living room. "What did you do?"

Dustin ran his hands over his head, his fingers tugging the hair, trying to yank the image of Trace crying from his brain. "Nothing."

"Then why did I cut my date short with Jewels because she received an SOS from Wind stating you'd done something to Trace? Dropped her off crying. Trace doesn't cry." Trevor held his keys tight in his fist, undoubtedly ready to handle this man-style. Dustin would take his lumps if that made his friend feel better. Heck, he'd lean in for a few blows.

Dustin dropped his hands to his knees and realized the image of Robert still illuminated his cell, so he quickly snagged it and hit the off button.

"What was that?" Trevor chuckled, but it wasn't a laugh of

humor. "Great. Some girl called, interrupting your date with Trace, and you ditched her?"

Dustin laughed, a deep, guttural, animal-dying kind of laugh. "Right, because Trace is that sensitive?"

The lights flickered and a boom sounded in the distance, warning of an approaching storm.

Trevor tossed his keys onto the table and then sat down. "I know you wouldn't do anything intentional to hurt Trace. Not since you turned a corner and realized she wasn't the enemy, but you had to have done something unintentionally."

Dustin didn't say anything. How could he? This was Trace's business, not his. He wouldn't betray her. Not to Wind and not to Trevor. "Believe what you want." He pushed from the couch and climbed the stairs to his little box he called a room. He'd gone from palatial penthouse to pocket-sized pantry.

Trevor followed him up the stairs. "Hey, man. Seriously. What happened? You look like you've been bullied and beaten."

"Nothing. Don't worry about me." Dustin reached his room.

"Wait. What should I tell Jewels? She's texting me, asking what I found out." Trevor held up his cell as if it were waiting for Dustin to speak directly into it.

"Tell her that Trace is a good woman who deserves better." Dustin shut the door on Trevor and any possibility of Trace in his life. This entire situation had been a fiasco since he'd arrived.

He couldn't go on like this. Tomorrow, he'd return to her father's place and work harder than he had ever worked in his life. They'd work together in silence. She'd hide behind the manual labor, and that would be okay with him. Because as much as he wanted to admit he could let her go, he'd do anything to see her again. He'd go and punch Robert in the nose if he had the chance. Something had to be done to help Trace understand it wasn't her fault, but what could he do, after swearing to silence?

CHAPTER NINETEEN

"COME ON, hon. Tell us what that evil man did to you." Wind settled on the side of the bed, but Trace faced the wall. She didn't want to talk about it. Any of it. What had she been thinking, telling Dustin?

Houdini cuddled up at her side and purred. His soft fur soothed her a bit.

"I'm sorry," Kat said in an un-Kat-like soft tone. "I thought I was so clever, pulling that deal out and making you both work together. It was stupid."

"You didn't do anything wrong," Trace mumbled into the pillow, longing to tell them everything, but she couldn't. She'd already opened her big mouth to Dustin. She couldn't bring her sisters into this nightmare, too. Besides, she could never let them know what she'd done.

Jewels patted her leg. "We're all here for you, hon."

"Even me," Bri said in her light and happy voice.

"Nothing any of you can do. I'm fine. Tired, that's all."

Jewels's hand rubbed small circles on Trace's back. Humiliation didn't begin to explain how she felt at this moment.

Crying was for the weak, girly girls who needed attention. Not her. She was the one who would console everyone else. This attention from her friends unnerved her, and she needed to escape this friend therapy. "Listen. I'm fine. Better than fine." She shot up and scooted to the edge of the bed. "As a matter of fact, I'm going to go work on my dad's place. I'll be back in a few hours."

Kat blocked her exit, all five foot ten inches of her. "Not going anywhere."

"Listen, leggy lawyer, get out of my way." Trace looked to the others when Kat didn't back down.

"We want to make sure you're okay. Running off to hide in your father's house isn't the answer." Jewels lifted Houdini to her shoulder and looked to Bri as if her daughter could find a better way to trap Trace in the room all night.

Bri scratched Houdini's head. "If Trace wants to go work out whatever is upsetting her, shouldn't we let her go? That's how Trace deals. Avoidance and hard work."

Trace didn't like being talked about like she wasn't even in the room. "Avoidance? I've taken on some of the biggest institutions in the world on my own or with little support. I've always attacked things directly, and I've never backed down." Until Matt's death.

Kat stepped out of her way. "We know you're keeping something from us, but we're here if you want to talk."

Trace grabbed a lantern from the room and bolted from house, the love of old friends. At a brisk pace, she made it to the edge of town, avoiding the path behind Trevor's place. Crying into Dustin's arms was embarrassment enough for one day.

Rhonda strutted out of Skip's and crossed the road. Trace

picked up the pace. "The town's going to see you for who you really are. I'll make sure of that."

Trace didn't stop. No way Rhonda knew anything about what happened on that oil rig. The company had paid big money to shut down the talk and avoid bad press. Gag orders issued. Threats implied. Guilt and fear used as tools to silence her.

Trace's breath came in short bursts, and her heart hammered against her ribs, but she didn't stop. Not until she closed herself off from the world in her father's home.

Her home.

She forced the anxiety into submission, flicked on the lanter, picked up a box, and tossed everything from the top shelf in the kitchen into it with one swoop of her arm. She opened up the cabinet under the sink and flung all the old cleaning chemicals into a bag. She yanked the 1970s fruit-faced clock from the wall and held it over the box but didn't let it go.

The sound of cars in the distance buzzed like an oboe, waves crashing against the retaining wall like cymbals, chirping of grasshoppers like a flute. Something was missing from the song of years past. She turned the old clock over and wound it.

Tick. Tick. Tick. Tick.

That sound completed the childhood symphony.

She retrieved from the shelf the book her father had left her and collapsed on the floor, setting the old clock by her side to tick away. "Dad, I'm sorry. I'm sorry for leaving you. I'm sorry for not visiting more. I'm sorry I'm not the woman you raised me to be."

For twenty wave crashes and four car passes, she remained on the floor, legs tucked under her. "I wish you were here. For decades when you were alive, I never needed you. Now that you're gone, I'd do anything to have you here. The guilt, regrets, are debilitating. I can't see through it to know what to do. I need to make this right, Dad. How do I move on with my life if I can't fix my past?"

She abandoned the book and clock to open the faux drawer in the desk to retrieve the letter. It was time. She needed to mail it. To tell the family what exactly happened to their son. What part she'd played in his death and the truth about the company that paid them off not to ask questions.

It didn't matter if they sued her. She didn't have much to take. A small retirement plan, but she didn't need much to survive in this world.

Prison. That would be horrible, but if physical jail meant freedom for her soul, she'd pay that price, too.

Still, something kept her from mailing that letter.

She yanked the drawer open and crushed the letter to her chest. The secret. The truth gnawed at her every thought. The weight of her deception pounded her into submission and silence. She thought it would be less now that she'd unburdened herself to Dustin, but all that had done was add to her fear of discovery.

How long could she keep the truth from the world? "Dad, what should I do?"

A light knock at the front door drew her from the past. She shoved the letter back into the drawer and opened the front door to see her three friends and Bri standing together.

Jewels lifted a pitcher of homemade margaritas, and Wind held out plastic glasses.

"You don't have to tell us anything. We only want to be here for you." Kat marched past her and plopped a radio onto the table.

Bri held Houdini up to Trace. "He wanted to come, too."

Houdini squawked at her as if in warning that he'd still be mischievous but he was here for her.

In that moment, she didn't feel so alone. Her lifelong friends by her side without pressuring her to share meant everything to her. Only, she *wanted* to share, but not with them.

Not because she didn't trust them. She trusted them more than anyone, but the warnings and threats from Robert's lawyers had stuck with Trace enough that she didn't want to risk any of them.

She picked up a box and went to work, allowing herself a reprieve from the monster memory of her failings.

That's what friendsters did, provided respite from life. She only hoped she didn't pull them under with her.

CHAPTER TWENTY

DUSTIN PACKED two coffees and waters and hope—hope of showing her that she didn't need to carry guilt or feel responsible for what had happened to her—into his bag and set off for Trace's place. They weren't right for each other, but that didn't mean he couldn't help her.

He stopped and put a sign on the hotel's main door, telling her he'd be at her place, and then took the short walk. It wasn't long enough to allow him much time to overthink what he'd tell her.

He didn't deserve her, but he wanted her. That was the problem. For the first time in his life, he needed to put someone else ahead of his own desires. She was good, despite what she thought. And the accident wasn't her fault. It was only that. An accident.

Would she listen?

He'd make her.

At the door, he knocked twice, but it didn't open. He was a few minutes early, so he set his supplies on the kitchen table and noticed everything had been packed and put in different areas of the house. She must've worked all night.

He would work as hard as she was to get this place ready for her to move back into it. The list of inspection items that Kat had provided pushed him to tackle the roof first.

A tall ladder at the side of the house gave him access to the roof. Unfortunately, it was worse than he'd first imagined. She needed an entirely new roof. He'd start by removing the shingles and tarping it until he could get roofers out here to put on a new one.

On his knees, arched over, he worked as the sun rose into the sky. No sign of Trace. He worried she'd never show, but he kept working. His arms burned from overuse and the sun that managed to sneak through the canopy by high noon.

Sweat poured down his body, and for a moment he thought about jumping into the ocean, but he wasn't that desperate. Still, he needed a break.

He didn't care that Trace was so late, but he worried she'd never come around him again. He'd go check the hotel to make sure she wasn't working there, but if he didn't find her there and she didn't show by midday, he'd go find her at Jewels's place. For the moment, he could stick his feet in the water and dump a bucket over his head. Sharks couldn't go in water that shallow, could they?

Outside, he trudged through the overgrown grass. He eyed the hotel, but there was no sign of Trace, so he headed to the beach near the dock. He could wade in to his knees, splash some water on himself, and then return to work.

At the edge of the ocean, he removed his work boots and socks. He waded in to his ankles. The cool water soothed his toes and feet. Ankle deep was progress. At this rate, he'd reach knee-deep by Christmas.

Something floated toward him in the water. He jumped back, sure it was a shark, but it wasn't. It was a paddleboard. One of Jewels's.

A shot of heat seared his body. His breath caught. Mouth went sand dry.

He scanned the water but didn't see anyone.

A splash rippled the waves, and he caught sight of blonde hair before it went under again.

He trembled at the sight. "Trace!"

No answer. No resurface. No Trace.

He didn't think. Didn't breathe. Didn't wait.

He dove into the water headfirst and swam like Michael Phelps.

"Trace!" No answer.

At the board, he reached around under the water and touched something. It bolted up out of the surf with a yelp.

He screamed.

Trace splashed and scraped her nails at him. He grabbed her around the waist and hoisted her up onto the board. She coughed and choked on the ocean water.

"Don't worry. I've got you." He held on to the board and kicked and kicked.

"What are you doing?" Trace managed between coughs.

"Rescuing you."

"From what? Practicing my freediving?"

He stopped kicking. "What?"

"I do that when I'm stressed or need to focus. It's my yoga equivalent." Trace shook her head. "Ah, you know you're in the ocean, right?"

His attention snapped from a distressed woman to surrounding sharks. The ones he couldn't see.

His heart beat faster than flying fish wings. Pulse hammered. Skin tingled.

He froze.

"Come on, knight in shining distress. I'll get you to shore." She slid off the board and kicked by his side, shoulder to shoulder toward the shore. "I guess you can swim."

"Never said I couldn't," he grumbled, scanning the water for fins. "Freediving, really? Aren't there tanks for that sort of thing?"

"Not scuba diving. It's only thirty feet in the middle of the channel. No need for a tank."

He wiped the stinging, salty water from his eyes. "There's every reason for a tank. What if you got trapped down there?"

"On what? Sand?" She laughed, but her teasing didn't bother him. He welcomed it—the distraction and the connection. "Looks like we have company."

He flinched, sure a fin protruded from the water and headed their way, but then he followed her finger to Trevor standing on the beach laughing.

"Told you she'd get you to do something crazy. I can't wait to see you in the pink apron mowing the lawn."

"That doesn't count. She didn't convince me to do anything. I jumped in because I thought she was drowning." When his toes brushed the sand underneath him, relief cooled his skin.

Trevor met them at the water's edge and offered a hand to Dustin. "Listen, I don't care how she did it. Just glad she did. Good job, Trace."

Dustin shook his head, shooting excess water to the ground. "Right. Great job."

Trace unstrapped the board from her ankle, and Trevor

took it. He set it against the side of the wooden post of the dock and laughed all the way back up the hill.

"Thank you," Trace said in an honest, soft tone.

"For what?"

She unzipped the shortie wetsuit and pulled her arms free, revealing a bathing suit that accentuated her chest and tight arms. His breath caught.

"For putting my safety above your fear." Trace studied the ground. "That took courage. I can't believe you did that for me. You're a good man."

His skin heated at her words. No, he'd never been a good man. Not that he was evil or unkind, just selfish. Had Trace brought out something different in him?

He stripped off his shirt and tossed it onto the dock and wrung out his shorts at the cuff. "It wasn't a big deal."

She hooked her fingers around his. "It was." Her gaze traveled from his eyes, to his lips, to his bare chest, and back to his lips.

In that moment, he wanted to kiss her. Kiss her and make her see that he could give her the world and she could be happy.

She took in a stuttered breath and looked up at him.

He leaned in.

She pressed her palm to his chest. "Wait. I need to share something with you."

Disappointment at her rejection took hold, but the way her thumb moved over his skin made him feel a longing he hadn't felt in years, if ever. Trace was a woman worth waiting for. He couldn't push her. He had to let her ease into something with him. And he had work to do to deserve her. "Okay. I'm listening."

She shook her head. "Not here. Follow me." After a glance

around the area as if to search out enemies in the bushes, she let him go and walked toward the trail to her place.

The separation forced a coldness inside him he couldn't explain in the ninety-plus degree temperature. All he could do was follow her.

At the edge of the woods, she didn't speak. At the edge of the house, she didn't speak. At the edge of a desk, she didn't speak.

She opened a drawer, popped open a hidden door, and retrieved an envelope. With the crumpled white letter held to her chest, she sat on the edge of the desk and closed her eyes. "I don't know if I can share this with you. I told you the basics, but this gives the details. An account of why I'm at fault. I'm sure you'll hate me after you read it, but I can't keep this to myself anymore, and I don't know what to do."

Dustin felt ripped in half between wanting to understand what she faced that kept them apart but at the same time dreading the knowledge. "What about Jewels, Wind, Kat, and Bri?"

She shot to her feet. "No. They can't know. You promised you wouldn't tell anyone. You can never say anything, or this could take you down, too."

Dustin longed to touch her, to still her trembling hands, to pull her into his arms and hold her until she calmed and hours after. "You can trust me."

"I know." Trace took in a long breath and then blew it out as if to free herself from poisonous gas. "A man willing to face his fears to save me is a man I have to trust, or I'll never trust anyone again." She mumbled something else, but all he caught was "Dad" and "sure."

She held out the envelope with her shaking hand, and he took it.

"Should I read it now?"

Trace nodded but took off for the back bedroom as if she couldn't face him as he read what darkness waited inside the folded paper. He leaned against the desk and opened the envelope, unfolded the paper, and scanned the note.

Dear Mr. and Mrs. Sanders,

I am writing to tell you more about your son. He was working for me the night he died. Matt was an amazing person who had a heart for all things living. He followed me into battle and courageously faced the bureaucratic enemies ravaging our environment.

That's what he believed, because that's what I told him.

This isn't easy for me to explain, but I wanted you to know that I take responsibility for your son's death. I've remained silent all this time in fear of the retaliation I'd face if I spoke up, but I can't keep the truth from you.

I'm aware that Remming Enterprises in conjunction with the Brazilian oil company paid you a substantial sum under the guise of goodwill despite your son's illegal actions, but they lied. Your son wasn't trying to sneak onto the rig that night to sabotage or to cause damage out of some misguided youthful notion he would be famous for his work as an extremist. Your son was there to gather photographic evidence of the illegal practices of the corporations running the rig.

I should've been with him to gather evidence, helping and ensuring his safety, but instead I was being manipulated by Mr. Remming with romance and empty promises. He told the authorities that I had a crush on him and he'd dissuaded me, despite my misguided attempts at winning his affections. Mr. Remming turned his deceit around and accused me of manipulating your son by using his desire to please me to convince him to perform the sabotage that got him killed.

None of this is true.

I've remained quiet, but despite the gag order the company and Brazilian government nudged me to sign in exchange for my freedom and a large settlement to you, I couldn't keep quiet any longer. You needed to know the truth, even if you don't believe me.

I'm sorry that I wasn't there for Matt. I'll carry that guilt with me the rest of my days. Ultimately, I take responsibility for his death because he was my intern, but I never and would never manipulate someone to destroy property. That is Remming Enterprise's MO, not mine.

Please accept my deepest condolences and my heartfelt apology for failing your son. If I could go back and sacrifice myself for Matt, I would.

Sincerely,
   Trace Latimer

Dustin lowered the paper and found Trace standing in front of him with a wild, fear-filled, wide-eyed gaze.

"Now you know the truth. It's my fault that Matt died."

He dropped the paper to the ground and cupped her cheek. "No. It's not. And I'll prove it to you."

"No. You promised." Trace grabbed his biceps, squeezing until her nails dug into his skin. "These people will ruin my friends and lie to everyone about me. I can't embarrass our town like that. I came home after promising to keep my mouth shut. They paid Matt's parents, who needed the money more than anyone. I thought I'd done the right thing at the time, but when I found out the company told them that their son had been there to commit sabotage and would've been put in jail, I couldn't keep the truth any longer."

141

Dustin bent over, resting his forehead on hers and willing her to hear the truth. "It wasn't your fault. I'll keep my promise. I would never betray you, but Trace, look at me." He nudged her chin so she'd have to face him and looked deep into her eyes, willing her to see the truth. "You need to forgive yourself for allowing that man to manipulate you. I know you'll never trust me when I say this, but I'm not Robert Remming, and I'd never use your feelings to get what I want."

She blinked and took shallow breaths. "I do. God help me, but I do believe you." She lunged into him, wrapping her arms around his neck and kissing him.

He stood, holding her tight, and kissed her back.

A kiss that shattered him. Broke him into a thousand pieces of nothing. But when she clung to him, the pieces glued back together. Together in a new way. A way that made him a better man, whole for the first time in his life.

CHAPTER TWENTY-ONE

T<small>RACE CLUNG TO</small> D<small>USTIN</small>. She forgot everything in the world except for his lips. He soothed the pain in her heart and replaced it with joy. A child's Christmas morning kind of joy.

Heat spread from her lips to her neck, over her shoulders, down her arms. His arms around her were like support beams for life.

They broke apart, panting and clinging to each other.

Passion. Heart-pumping, mind-numbing, oh-so-good passion.

"I've got you," he whispered, lowering her back to her feet but not letting go.

Trace pressed her cheek to his chest. "You don't hate me?" She wanted to know but feared the truth.

"Never," he whispered and pressed his lips to her head. "I'll support you in any way you would like. I'll fight the giants. I've got the money stored away to hire lawyers for you. I'll scream from the rooftops that there's no way you would've risked anyone's life. I'll protect you from the media. I'll hire a hitman for Robert Remming. Better yet, I'll take care of him myself. Tell me what you need, and I'll do it."

"Hold me. Don't judge me. Keep my secret." She wrapped her arms around his middle and held on. "I don't know what I'm going to do, but it helps that I'm not alone anymore. That someone knows the truth."

"You're not alone. I'm sorry you've had to carry this with you for so long. It's not fair." He rubbed her back. "You did nothing wrong."

"I allowed myself to turn my back on everything I knew because of some guy. Matt saw us kissing. That's why he took off into the ocean. Not to save the sea creatures, but to save me from Robert. To show me the truth about his manipulation and illegal actions."

"Shhh. It isn't your fault. I'll say it a hundred times, a thousand, enough until you believe it."

"If I mail the letter, I need to leave. You can have the house. I can't save it or make up for not being here for my father, but I can protect this town when the media discovers my part in all this."

Dustin stiffened. "No. Stay. I'm so sorry about fighting you on this house. I thought you were a different person who only wanted to thwart my attempts out of spite."

"Rhonda made you believe that."

"You mean I was manipulated by a woman with some alternate agenda? I'm a horrible person."

Trace leaned back and smacked him in the belly. "Not the same thing."

He took hold of her face with such gentleness, she felt cherished and cared for. "It is, Trace. It's exactly the same thing, and if you blame yourself, then I need to take responsibility for what I did."

"Will it help if I said I forgive you?" Trace said, but the distraction of his lips so close dizzied her.

"Only if you can forgive yourself."

Trace sighed. "It isn't that easy. You almost cost me a home. I cost a man his life." She pulled away, knowing she couldn't stay in Dustin's arms a minute longer and remember the facts. And she refused to be steered in the wrong direction. "I need to figure out if I should send that letter or not. If I do, I could be reopening Matt's parents' wounds. If I do, I could risk this house, my friends, this town...you."

"Don't worry about me." Dustin's hands were on her shoulders, almost making her believe he could fix this for her.

"If I don't send it, I-I..."

"Will never allow yourself to move on with your life." Dustin snuck his hands around her and pulled her against him. "Then you should send it. You should tell the world what really happened. That Robert Remming is a bully. If I know Trace Latimer, she doesn't back down from a fight and would never let a bully win. Tell the girls. They'll tell you the same thing."

Trace spun around on him. "No. You promised. The girls can't know."

He held up his hands. "Okay, I won't. I'm only saying that you should."

The sound of the clock ticking in the kitchen soothed her but also made her remember how this town and her friends saw her. "I'll be exposed to the world. Rhonda's right. The town will finally know who I really am. A girl who abandoned her father. A self-proclaimed do-gooder who didn't need any luxuries in life. A person who chose fight over family, only to be the woman who put herself over everything."

Twigs cracked outside, drawing Trace to the open window

in time to spot a bunny hopping across the ground. She returned to the desk, folded the letter, and tucked it away in its home before picking up Dustin's tool belt and heading toward the door. "For now, we both have a job to do. No more standing around slacking. Get to work."

Dustin met her at the doorway, blocking her exit. "Fine, but tell me that you won't handle this alone. Let me fix this for you. I can—"

"Stay out of it. Don't make me regret telling you." She squared her shoulders and stared him down like a killer whale to a seal.

He backed out of her way and grabbed the tool belt from her. "You can work down here while I finish the roof."

"Oh, no. We had a deal. Let's head to the hotel."

"Hotel is supposed to be in the morning—says so in Kat's documents."

"I wasn't there to help you this morning."

"The hotel can wait. I want your house finished."

"A deal's a deal. Besides, when you finish the hotel, you'll have a reason to stay in Summer Island with Trevor and Jewels."

He swooped her up into his arms once more. "I've already found a reason to stay."

Trace squirmed in his arms, not because she wanted to get away but because she feared she'd never let him go.

* * *

FOR A WEEK, they worked side by side down the list Kat had provided them. Mornings in the hotel, afternoons at the house, evenings on the beach tucked away around the corner where prying eyes couldn't watch. Each night, Trace had to peel herself away and return to Jewels's place.

In that week, she began to believe anything was possible with Dustin by her side. On the eighth day, she rose from bed with Houdini curled up on her pillow and went to make coffee like every other morning.

"Does she know?" Kat asked in a conspirator tone.

Trace paused at the edge of the hallway at the unexpected sound of her friend's voice at this hour.

"Do you think she spoke to the press and not us?" Wind asked.

A jolt of warning seared Trace's skin.

"No," In a tone that said Jewels didn't believe that.

Trace shuffled into the kitchen, and Bri snagged a newspaper off the table, folded it, and shoved it under her arm. "Good morning."

"What's going on?" Trace looked between them.

Kat crossed her arms, and her lip curled at the edge. "Why didn't you tell us?"

Wind smacked her.

"Tell you what?" Trace rubbed her eyes free of sleep.

Jewels held out her hand to Bri, who relinquished the newspaper. "About this." She plopped it down on the table.

"They still print those things? I thought everything was digital."

"The *Summer Island Gazette* still prints and delivers." Kat jabbed her finger at the paper. "You spoke to the press and not us? That's what you've been stewing and upset about?"

In large print, the headline read, *Tree hugger or Murderer: Small-Town Activist Caused Big-Time Problems.*

Fire surged through her veins. "He didn't." She snagged the paper and skimmed the article. Everything in her letter, everything she'd told Dustin, printed for the world to see. "I'll kill him."

She bolted out of the kitchen, out of the house, and down the beach to Trevor's house. With her fist balled tight, she pounded on the glass sliding door, sure it would shatter.

"What are you doing? You're not even dressed, hon," Wind shouted, running up the hill holding out a robe.

Trevor came down the stairs and opened the door. "What's going on? What did Dustin do now?"

Trace shoved the paper into Trevor's gut. "Dustin!" she shouted.

"He's not here. He's in town." Trevor eyed the paper. "I don't understand."

She turned around in the circle of prying judgmental eyes. "It's true. All of it. I was the cause of Matt's death, and Dustin was the only one who knew the entire story. The story he promised never to share."

Trace pushed past her friends, past the pain, past the hope, and marched to town to face the lying, soul-crushing Dustin Hawk.

CHAPTER TWENTY-TWO

"RHONDA, you need to understand. I'm only trying to smooth things over so that both you and Trace can live in this town peacefully. Isn't it time to let go of the past to embrace the future?" Dustin nudged the contract he'd had Kat draw up last night allowing Rhonda beach access free of charge at his resort during low and mid-season.

"Why would I do that? It's Trace who should be here apologizing to me and this town. She's a fake, you know. I can't believe you fell for her holier-than-an-angelfish attitude."

He didn't know what that meant, but he wasn't going to challenge her metaphor at the moment. "Tell me why you want to tear down her home."

"Not her home. It's her father's, and she wasn't around when he died. Do you know who was? Me." She impaled her chest with her thumb. "I'm the one who took him food from here." She waved her hand around the ship-like wooden room of Skip's restaurant. "I'm the one who picked up after him."

"I didn't realize you were helping him before he passed." Dustin wanted to make things right, and in that moment he remembered that there were two sides to every story and obviously Rhonda wanted to be heard. "Tell me about his final days. You must've gotten close to him in the end."

She shrugged and dropped her hand to the table. "I thought so, but I guess not."

"Why's that?" Dustin asked in a counselor tone.

She slammed her palm down with a smack that echoed around the restaurant. Two people eating their fish and chips in the corner watched them. "Trace wasn't around. I came to his house daily for a year. I should've inherited his place, not her. I was more of a daughter to him than she has ever been."

Dustin fought his instinct to defend Trace. If Rhonda knew what she'd been through, maybe she'd back down. "Deep down, you understand that Trace was his daughter. No matter how much you cared for him, in the end, family obligation wins. It may not be fair, but it is the law."

"He didn't leave me anything. Nothing. Not even that old clock in the kitchen. I'd wind that thing daily for him. For some reason, he liked the sound. It's as if he never cared about me. Fathers are supposed to care, even if my bio dad never did. I thought..." Her voice faded.

He understood now that Rhonda hadn't tried to tear down the old house out of spite or some childhood feud. She'd been hurt. She was lashing out because she'd believed she meant more to Trace's father than he'd indicated after leaving everything to his daughter. "You deserved better than that. Maybe I can get that clock for you." Dustin reached out and patted her hand, a sign of a friend or confidant.

"Trace won't like that," Rhonda said in a conspiratorial tone.

He wasn't going to engage in any conversation about Trace, so with his free hand, he scooted the document across the table. "This gives you what you wanted. Access to the beach. Read it over. Have your lawyer look over it. There's even a place in here about clearing the edge of the hotel property so you can have an unobstructed view of the beach from your house. And of course, the shed shack in the woods will be torn down."

"Really?" She raised an eyebrow at him. "What will Trace say?"

His pulse flipped and fluttered, but in the end, he hoped Trace would understand that he'd done this for peace in her life. If he couldn't fight the big oil whale, he could at least take on the minnow in the pond. "You let me worry about Trace."

"Where is he?" A raving, half-dressed Trace entered Skip's place. Her soldier-behind-enemy-lines gaze shot through him with such intensity, it knocked the wind from his lungs. He snatched his hand instinctively from Rhonda, who shoved the contract back at him.

"Keep your fancy words. I know you're not my friend." The way she smiled like a devil dancing around the depraved made his skin crawl. "If it isn't Ms. Murderer." Rhonda sauntered up to Trace with an air of Mother Teresa Superiority. "Now everyone knows the liar you are."

Murderer?

Trace lifted her hand, but Kat and Wind jumped in front of her.

Dustin rushed to her side and faced Rhonda, making sure that Trace knew he'd always take her side. "You need to leave. I made you a fair offer. It's up to you what you do with it."

Rhonda snickered. "I know exactly what I'm going to do with it." She shot past them and disappeared out the door.

Dustin reached for Trace, but she stepped away. A small step with a Grand Canyon-sized ravine between them. Her eyes were wide and wild, breath short and stuttered. "You! How could you?"

Tears pooled in her eyes, but they didn't spill down her cheeks.

Dustin looked at her, to the girls, to the others in the restaurant, but couldn't find the answer to his sin. "What are you talking about?" He looked to Kat. "Oh, she told you?"

Trace looked to Kat, who only shook her head. "Told me what? That I trusted the wrong man? Why? Why'd you do it?"

"I was trying to help. She won't get any of your property. Only mine." Dustin tried to gather her into his arms, to soothe her anger, but she pressed a newspaper into his chest and shoved him away. He snatched the coarse, crinkled heap before it hit the floor. On the front page, he saw it. The reason for Trace's meltdown.

"How?" He skimmed the article.

"You. You're the only one who knew anything about this. I'll be taken to court. I'll lose what little I have. All because of you. The least you can do is tell me why." Trace stumbled back, but the girls were there to catch her.

His gut knitted into a knot. A tight, constricting knot. "You don't think that I…?" He shook his head, willing her to listen to him. "I would never!"

Trace waved her arms in the air and turned in a circle with the robe open and her nightgown flowing around her. A vision of tortured beauty. "Then who? You were the only one I told. I didn't even tell my friends. No one else knew."

Acid churned and clawed its way up his throat, spilling the putrid taste into his mouth. "I don't know. But it wasn't me."

Trace bit her bottom lip. Her angry, tight face melted into a loose sorrow. "You were the only one. The only one I trusted."

He tossed the paper to the side and stepped toward her, but Jewels scooted between them. "No. I don't know what's going on, but not here. Not now."

Bri moved to her mother's side. "You don't get to speak with her again. Not now, not ever."

Kat and Wind joined them, surrounding Trace in an impenetrable friendship fort. They ushered her out of his reach, out of his sight, out of his life.

CHAPTER TWENTY-THREE

TRACE ROWED out to Friendship Beach. The one place she knew no one would bother her. The little island across the channel that had been their haven as children and now her respite place as an adult.

News trucks poured into their sleepy little town when the *Tampa Tribune* reprinted the *Summer Island Gazette* article online. It swooped through the cities and hit the news broadcasts in two days.

If it weren't for Houdini chewing a camera wire to distract the crew, she would've never made her escape through the back fence unnoticed. Houdini was the best.

Stroke after stroke helped calm her nerves while crossing the channel. At the canal, she turned in, ducking beneath overgrown mangroves. At the beach, she dismounted the board and dragged it up on shore.

The movement, the exercise, kept her mind busy, but when she crossed the small peninsula to the lagoon side, she could see the edge of the dock and the boats and the beach bordering Dustin's life.

Her chest throbbed. She rubbed her sternum, as if rubbing the notion of the almost-relationship with the wrong man from her heart.

It didn't work.

The anguish infested her with spikes of sadness and claws of cruelty. Cruelty that Dustin had posed as a man with compassion, caring for her feelings, when all the time he only used her. For what, she couldn't reconcile. None of it made sense.

All she knew was that she'd been manipulated into believing a man again. She had no one to blame but herself.

She'd been blind, but she needed to wake up and fix this.

But how?

How could she make something right in her story when Robert Remming controlled the narrative?

The sound of a marine engine revved her pulse to rocket speed. She ducked into the mangroves and peered through the branches. To her relief, Kat and Jewels were on Trevor's dingy. There was no sign of Dustin or the press or Rhonda or any other enemy.

"Trace. It's only us." Jewels lifted the engine, and they both paddled to the beach through the shallow canal. "We need to tell you something."

Kat hopped out and tied the dinghy line to the post Trevor and Jewels had installed a few months ago.

Trace traipsed out of the trees and faced her friends. "I came here to be alone. To think."

The water rippled onto the shore and then retreated back into the dark canal that Trace wished she could disappear into. The water had always been her barrier to pain.

"You can return to your self-brooding after our chat. But you need to know something first."

"Is it that important that it couldn't wait until I returned?"

Kat popped a hip out and took on her attorney persona with shoulders back, chin up, attitude out. "You think I'd come out here if it wasn't?"

Trace picked up a stone and skidded it across the water of the lagoon. It hit one of the rocky outcroppings that kept their little island paradise from tourist boats and then sank. "Fine. What is it?"

"I know a way out of all of this." Kat marched across the sand and stood by Trace's side.

A boat came tearing through the channel, ignoring the no-wake zone, sending waves up through the lagoon onto shore, tickling Trace's toes. "How are you going to shut up the media, convince the world that the lonely murderess wasn't at fault, and tell me how the man I loved didn't stab me in the back?"

"Love?" Jewels joined them.

"No. I didn't mean that. I meant trust. We were friends."

Jewels opened her mouth to say more, but Kat's quick reflexes shot out with an arm and a look. "Listen. I can't fix everything, but I can fix the legal side. You signed a gag order —which was stupid."

"You can chastise me later."

"Right, well... You broke the gag order and that's illegal," Kat grumbled.

"I didn't mean to. I told one person, and he told the world."

Kat shook her head. "You still told someone. And it wasn't us."

Trace realized she'd hurt Kat's feelings and probably the rest of her friends as well. "I couldn't tell you guys. I couldn't wrap you up in my mess. I did this. I needed to figure out how to handle it."

"But you told Dustin." Jewels pushed Trace's hair behind her ear. "I don't believe he told anyone."

"He's the only one who knew. I was at my breaking point. I didn't know what to do, and he was there."

"We were there," Kat said with clipped speech.

"I told you. I couldn't have risked it."

"You could've hired me as your attorney for guidance," Kat hissed. "It would've been legal to tell me in confidence."

Trace wasn't sure if Kat was madder at her because she didn't trust her as a friend or a lawyer. "I hadn't thought about that. All I thought about was the guilt that I'd kept the secret of how a family's son died and how it was my fault that he was there that night."

Her words lodged in her throat. She choked down the tears before they could take hold.

Jewels hugged her into her side. "I'm so sorry you've gone through this without us."

"I was desperate. I'd even written a letter to the family and thought about mailing it. I showed the letter to Dustin. That's how I know it was him who gave the information to the newspaper. Only someone who read that letter would know the details."

"He wouldn't do that. Trevor swears he didn't even tell him. He kept the secret for you," Jewels said.

"Letter? What letter?" Kat asked as if she hadn't heard anything else she'd said.

"The letter I wrote explaining—"

"I got that part. Where's that letter now?" Kat asked.

Trace pointed across the channel. "Dad's place. Desk, faux compartment. No one would find it there."

Kat abandoned Trace's side.

"Where are you going?"

"To prove you're not liable." Kat untied the dinghy.

Trace took off after her. "Wait, how are you doing that?"

"Don't leave without me." Jewels took the tiller, Trace snuggled down in the middle, and Kat pushed them out into the canal.

"We're going to prove that letter was seen by someone else. An alternate crime was committed, and at worst you were negligent. However, I have a feeling the company won't want to take it that far. Not when we can countersue for gross negligence on their part.

Trace wasn't sure what all that meant, but she liked the direction they were taking. The only problem was, even if Kat could save her from a lawsuit, fines, and jail time, she couldn't save her from a broken heart.

CHAPTER TWENTY-FOUR

DUSTIN PUSHED his way through the crowds in town, marched into the *Summer Island Gazette,* and slammed his fist down on the front desk. "Tell me who gave you the scoop on the Robert Remming oil death and lied about Trace's part in it."

"I can't reveal my source," the man with a tuft of hair that fell over his forehead like a palm leaf touted.

People congregated in and around the newspaper office.

"I know Trace didn't tell you anything. And due to this source of yours, she's facing a lawsuit, public humiliation, and years of suffering. Tell me now, or I'm going out there to tell those reporters that you lied."

A tall, thin man with a cane joined them. "Hello, I'm Mr. Shelling. I am the owner and editor of the *Summer Island Gazette.* I assure you that we will not divulge any sources." He pointed to the mob outside. "However, I'm happy to report anything Ms. Latimer can tell me about the event. She can tell her side of the story."

"No. Never. What part of a gag order don't you under-stand? That's how I know she didn't tell anyone. She never would. This is all fantasy with no proof, and I for one will make sure she sues this paper until you're living out of a cardboard box on the beach."

"Mr. Hawk, I'm afraid that won't happen. I have proof." He lifted his chin. "Now, if you don't mind, I have an appointment to speak with the *New York Times*. Good day."

Dustin wanted to reach across the desk and yank the guy out of the building by his thin, short tie, but it wouldn't do any good. This was Mr. Shelling's fifteen minutes of fame, and he wasn't going to let it go. "So much for small-town love and loyalty." He bolted out, pushed through the crowd, and headed to Trevor's place to figure out a plan. There had to be something he could do to help. To show Trace it wasn't him.

At the edge of Hammerhead Drive, he took a breath of cleansing ocean air and continued walking to the house, where he eyed the sparkling ocean. He heard Trevor talking to someone inside. "I know Dustin wouldn't do it. I've known the man almost all my life."

Dustin entered and closed the glass sliding door behind him, sealing out the white noise of the ocean and birds and media.

"Right. Keep me updated. That has to be it." Trevor exited the kitchen and stopped short at the sight of Dustin. "Oh, when did you get here?"

"Just now. What has to be it?" Dustin asked, hope tickling his mood.

"There was a letter. Kat thinks that could be the key to getting Trace out of legal trouble."

"How?" Dustin asked, already backing toward the door.

Trevor shook his head. "Stay out of it, man. I know you didn't do anything wrong, but give Trace space to figure this out."

"I can't sit by and wait while my world falls apart. She has to believe me. I saw it in her eyes. She wanted to believe me."

"Was that before or after her friends pulled her out of Skip's before she could attack you?" Trevor slid his cell phone into his pocket and opened the door. "I can see there's no stopping you, so come on. We'll meet them at Trace's father's place."

Dustin darted out the door and jogged to the path. He didn't stop until he reached the front door and spotted the girls inside.

"It's gone!" Trace stood with the desk drawer and her mouth open.

Trevor reached his side, panting.

Dustin burst into the little house. "That's it. Someone found that letter and took it."

Trace slammed the desk drawer shut. Squirrels and rabbits skittered across the yard. Dustin looked to the window at the rustling. No sticks cracking. "Wait." He peered out the window and remembered their conversation that day and the snapping of twigs. Then the conversation with Rhonda at the table about how she'd been let down and how she didn't look surprised about the news. "I know who it was."

"Who?" Kat asked.

Dustin looked to Trevor, to Jewels, then to Trace. All of them looked at him like he held a snake in his hands. "Rhonda."

"Obviously," Wind said, waving her hands in the air. "We all suspect her, but we don't know she did it."

"Yes, we do. The way she acted at Skip's this morning. She already knew about the paper." He studied Trace, the way she moved and looked at him like a woman on the pier waving her sailor off to go to war. Torn. Torn between giving in to how he knew—or at least hoped—she felt about him and the fear of another betrayal.

"We have no proof," Kat said in a grave tone. "Without proof, this could go on for years in the court system. We need some sort of confession from her."

"But she'll never admit to this," Bri said.

Wind nodded her agreement. "We'll have to trick her somehow."

"I'll testify to what she said at Skip's this morning," Dustin offered.

"You'd do that for me?" Trace asked, sending hope shooting through his veins.

"Yes. I'd do anything to make this right. I'll help fix this." He nudged closer. His breath caught, his mouth was dry, and his hands shook. "If you'll give me the chance."

CHAPTER TWENTY-FIVE

DUSTIN STOOD in front of her asking for too much. Heat seared Trace from the inside out. What should she do?

Robert had tricked her into falling for him, only to discover that he'd used her to push deals through while keeping her distracted. A distraction that cost Matt's life. She had to take responsibility for what happened. "No. You can't help. Only I can make this right."

She lifted her chin, but Dustin took her by the hands. "Listen to me. You're not alone. You have your friends, and you have me. Stop trying to push us all away."

"You still want to be with me? I accused you of betraying me."

"Yes."

He said it with such conviction, she wanted to believe him. A man who would state such fact in front of her friends had to be telling the truth, right? Still, something held her back. "You can't help. Please, don't get any more involved. Kat will represent me in court. If we need you as a witness, I'm sure she'll call you."

"And I'll be there." He turned to Kat but didn't let Trace go. His touch was like aloe on sunburned skin. "If we can get a confession out of someone for giving the letter to the newspaper, then she'll be okay?"

Kat nodded. "Better. There may still be some legal issues, but that would make a huge difference."

Dustin let her go, leaving her standing in a crowd of loneliness. Her friends were everything to her, but he'd taken her heart, and she couldn't get it back. He was the man she'd thought Robert was. For all the lies he'd told, Dustin had already told her the truth. A hollowness remained inside her.

"I'll take care of this," he said and then bolted out of the house at full speed.

Trace blinked and looked to Trevor for answers. "What's he going to do?"

"My guess? The man I know who has completely fallen for you, who could never stand by and let someone he cares about suffer? I'd say he went to confess."

"Confess?" Her stomach rolled like a tidal wave crashing into her gut. "He said he didn't—"

"He didn't. But that doesn't mean he won't give a false confession if it means saving you." Trevor took Jewels by the hand as if he couldn't face any of this without her.

"How do you know?" Trace asked, her pulse hammering so loudly she thought she wouldn't be able to hear his response, but it came in like a foghorn in the night. "Because it's what I would do." He kissed Jewels on the cheek.

Trace looked to Jewels, to Bri, to Wind, to Kat. None of them said a word. "I've got to stop him."

Kat pressed her lips together the way she did when she was processing an outcome in a court case. "You better do it fast before he makes things worse with a false confession."

Trace raced out of the house. She didn't need to look back to know her friends followed her. At the edge of town, Kat split off into Skip's place, and the rest stayed by her side and helped her push through the impromptu press conference outside the courthouse. Dustin spoke with animated hands from the front steps.

"Wait. Stop!"

The crowd didn't let her through, so she pushed and shoved until she realized that she'd never make it in time. If she was right, the mob cared about one thing. A firsthand account of the dirty details, and Trace would be the best one to give it. "I'm Trace Latimer."

The cameras turned on her like a hungry eel. People parted, allowing her access to the stage. Dustin tried to nudge her off the steps, but she only grabbed hold of his arm. "I believe you. Now it's your turn to trust me."

His gaze danced from her to the crowd and back to her. "I've got this. I won't let you go through any more. You've been through enough."

"No. I need to do this. If I'm ever going to be free, then I need to speak about what happened."

"But the gag order..." Dustin caressed her cheek with a longing gaze that took her back to the house in the sticky afternoon when she'd confessed and he'd comforted her, kissed her. Now more than ever, she wanted more of those kisses. "It's time for you to trust me."

He kissed her on the cheek, sending waves of want down her neck, but now wasn't the time. She needed to focus on getting them out of this if she ever hoped to have a future with Dustin.

He held her hand, never leaving her side.

"I know you're all here because you want to know more

dirt about the accusations made in the *Summer Island Gazette*," she said.

The crowd roared, flinging questions at her like grenades.

She didn't say anything again, waiting for the ravenous vultures to calm down. It took several minutes until they realized she wouldn't speak unless they were quiet.

"I will tell you now that I never spoke to the newspaper, nor any other news outlet about this. I didn't even tell my friends, even when the truth of what happened ate away at me until I almost crumbled. The gag order is in place. I have not violated it, and I won't violate it now. If this goes to court, I'll have a lot more to say if the judge instructs me to break said order. For now, go home. There isn't anything else to say."

Dustin held her tight and leaned in so she could hear him. "Are you sure about this? What if the company comes after you?"

"Then I'll do what Kat suggested. I'll tell the family everything and support them in a wrongful death suit." She took him by the hand and led them down the steps, pushing through the crowd until they spotted Wind waving her arms outside Skip's place.

Jewels and Trevor ushered them inside to find Rhonda and Skip and some suits standing together, along with Mr. Shelling.

Dustin tucked her into his side in that protective way of his, and she didn't want to push free. "What's going on?" he asked.

"We spoke to Robert Remming, and he agreed that if you silence the person who leaked the information, they won't press charges."

"How are we going to get Rhonda to shut her mouth?" Trace asked.

Rhonda snarled. "It wasn't me."

"If it wasn't you, then—"

Skip grunted. "I overheard you talking when I came to make an offer on your father's house. I decided I would end this feud between you girls by giving my daughter what she wanted and getting you away from her place. I knew it was a fool's mission, but when I heard what happened, I knew I could force you out when the town discovered your past."

Trace shook her head. "Why do you want me gone so badly?"

Rhonda stepped forward as if leading an assault. "Because I was the one who took care of your father the last year. That place should've been mine. No contract that boy toy of yours offered me is going to change that. Some beach access instead of owning that lot? That wasn't fair. Your dad should've left his place to me."

Trace wanted to yell at Rhonda, tell her how wrong she'd been, but she couldn't because she knew there was truth to her words. "You're right. It isn't fair."

All her friends snapped their attention to her.

"That being said, it's my childhood home. Yes, I was gone for too long. Yes, I should've been home when my father needed me, but I didn't know he was sick. He kept it from me. If someone had told me, I would've come home. If you were taking care of him, why didn't you tell me?"

Wind tsked. "Because she took care of him in hopes he'd leave the property to her. If you came back, that couldn't happen."

"No. That's not it."

"Then what?" Trace wanted to understand.

"He's the only father who ever gave a rat's tail about me. I wanted him to myself."

Trace didn't know if she wanted to hit the woman or hug her. She could stand there and continue to argue with Rhonda, yell at her for stealing her final hours with her father away from her, but that wouldn't help either of them. She was tired of fighting and feeling guilty. "I'm sorry if I haven't been kind to you in the past. I won't sell my father's place, but I can cut down some trees to give you a better view."

"Dashing Dustin already tried that," Rhonda grunted and shot out of the restaurant.

Trace knew it would take more than one conversation to mend old wounds. Especially ones that had been festering for three decades. For now, she had to face the situation in front of her. "If Skip confessed, does that mean I won't be sued?"

The suits whispered between themselves and Kat. Once they were done, Kat looked at Trace and said, "If you tell the press it was all a lie, then they'll back down."

She eyed the front window where camera lenses were pressed to the glass. Reporters shouted questions through the closed and locked front door. "No," Trace said, realizing she wasn't scared of the lawyers or the fines or the world knowing how she'd contributed to Matt's death, because in protecting herself, she'd given Robert Remming and his company what they wanted. "I won't lie. I'm not scared of the suits or what people think about me anymore, because that means I gave up the big fight against the giants who pick on the world. The fight that Matt took on alone when I wasn't there to help. It might be too late, but I owe it to Matt. I won't remain silent any longer."

Kat stared at her. Trace readied for a fight, but instead Kat opened her arms and hugged her. "Good. I'll help you fight." She slipped away as fast as she'd embraced her, leaving Trace to face one last obstacle.

Her own heart. The one that had kept Dustin at a distance.

She turned to face him, and in front of her friends, the press, the world, she wrapped her arms around Dustin Hawk and kissed him.

This time it wasn't a kiss to chase away the demons and end her pain. It was a kiss to show him how she felt and to start a new life with him. A man that was all wrong: a business bureaucrat with a cocky walk who's afraid of the ocean.

She fell into him, releasing all inhibitions. The passion rose inside her. The cameras clicking away faded. The gasps and giggles faded. The people and the world faded. All the people except Dustin.

When she finally felt her toes hit the ground again, she wobbled.

He kept her upright and pressed his head to hers. "You're like no other woman, Trace Latimer, and I never want to leave your side."

She settled and found her balance and slapped him on the shoulder. "Great. I'm thinking about going to swim with the sharks tomorrow."

Dustin tensed. "Nope. Not happening. I have other plans for you tomorrow."

"What's that?"

"You haven't helped with the hotel enough. You owe me." Dustin took her by the hand and led her out of Skip's and down the road with a trail of reporters following them. But she didn't care because she could handle any fight with her friends and Dustin by her side.

EPILOGUE

THE QUIET ON Friendship Beach welcomed the girls to their five different-colored chairs. Bri spread out the blanket, Wind the daiquiris, Jewels the sunscreen, and Trace the copies of *Anne of Green Gables*. Sun bathed her in warmth, and she relaxed, welcoming book club and conversation.

Wind poured a drink and handed it to Trace. "Toast to the free girl."

"I wouldn't go that far, but I did hear from Matt's parents, thanking me for coming out with the truth. I told them they should thank Kat for figuring out how I was able to come forward without ending up in more trouble." Trace took a sip of her sugary beverage, her arms and legs relaxed from their months of tight tension.

Kat plopped down in the red chair. "You're welcome. This would've been easier if you'd come to me in the first place."

Trace drew a line in the sand with her toes. "I think I didn't want you all to know what happened. I was embarrassed. I'm an almost fifty-year-old woman, and I was tricked by some man."

"Please, we've all suffered that ailment, hon." Wind twirled, her beach cover-up ballooning out around her, and handed Jewels a drink. "Except this one who gets it right every time."

Jewels lifted her glass. "Lucky, I guess. What about you? I hear you were spotted with your old high school sweetheart, Damon Reynolds."

"Hush, now. That's only rumor." Wind poured another daiquiri and handed it to Kat. "But what I know isn't a rumor? I heard one amazing lawyer speaking with a man about marriage."

Kat choked and coughed, red liquid dripping from her lips.

Wind laughed, pouring a drink for herself and settling into her own chair. "Told you so."

Jewels sat forward. "Is this true? Are there wedding bells in your future? When can we meet him? What's his name?"

"No. Never. Not telling." Kat dabbed at her lips and scowled at Wind. "I think I'm actually going to hang out here for a while anyway."

"Is that to avoid your partner turned lover turned marriage proposal?" Wind said loudly enough for the fisherman across the river to hear.

Kat rested her drink on the chair arm and narrowed her gaze at Wind. "Do you have a tap on my phone or something?"

"Nope. A secret sleuth. Houdini told me," Wind said as if that was enough.

"I think you've been injected one too many times with filler," Kat grumbled.

"It's true. You got up to get water the other day, and Houdini hopped up and pointed at your laptop. I went to investigate, and what did I see? A passionate, loving email promising to love you forever if you'd have him." Wind stood and held open her arms for dramatic flair.

"He's one crazy little ferret," Bri said with a chuckle.

"Email?" Trace tsked. "I'd think he'd be more romantic than that."

"We're lawyers," Kat said, as if that explained it all. Then she abruptly changed the subject. "I thought we were here to talk about *Anne of Green Gables*." She retrieved the book and held it up. "Did you figure out why your dad left this for you?

Trace eyed the book in her lap and then looked to Kat. "I think so. It was Dad's way of telling me that he understood I was different than most people in town and that he wanted me to follow my dreams and be someone who mattered to the world and myself."

Jewels reached out, touching her arm. "And he told me once that you were what he'd always dreamed of being but never had the courage to pursue. I think that's why he didn't send for you. He never wanted to get in your way."

"I wish he had, but I know that not sending for me wasn't because he didn't love me. He did it because he loved me more than anything in his life. Dustin made me see that when we were going through my father's things. My father had saved every little trinket that I ever made or gave to him growing up." Trace held the book to her chest as if to hug her memory of him.

They sat around Friendship Beach, chatting, sipping their drinks, and watching the boats go by. *Anne of Green Gables* turned out to be the perfect read. Trace submerged herself in the conversations of their youthful indiscretions and how each of them had a little Anne with an E in them. But she was the redheaded orphaned girl without the red hair. The too skinny, short-tempered, high-energy girl who grew up to be an activist her friends were proud of.

The sun dipped below the trees on the other side of Banana River, driving them to leave their book club behind and return to the world before the mosquitoes assaulted them.

At the edge of Trevor's dock, he and Dustin stood waiting for them.

Trace took Dustin's hand and followed him to the end. "I thought you wouldn't come out this far over the water?"

"For you I will." He reached into his pocket and handed her his phone. "They won."

"What?"

She glanced down to find a text from one of the attorneys he'd hired to represent Matt's family.

We received a settlement without going to court. Remming Enterprises has received hefty fines and will no longer be allowed to partner with the Brazilian oil company. Also, their stocks are plummeting from the bad publicity. Rumors are that Robert Remming is filing for bankruptcy.

"It's over?" Trace looked up at him.

"Yes." He pulled her into his arms and held her tight, making her believe in the world and herself again. "But it's just beginning for us."

She raised onto her toes. "I'd say we're in the middle."

"You'd tell me the sky was black if I said it was blue."

"Can you handle my challenges?"

He leaned over, his lips hovering over hers. "I embrace them and you." He kissed her, and she knew that today, tomorrow, and for the rest of her days, she'd be happy because she had found real love and friends and purpose at home in Summer Island, where new beginnings and happy endings were guaranteed.

．　．　．

THE END

SHRIMP PO'BOY

Ingredients

- 1/3 cup egg substitute
- 1/2 cup Panko bread crumbs
- 2 tablespoons Magic Shrimp Seasoning (or your favorite)
- 1 pound uncooked shrimp (16-20 per pound), peeled and deveined
- 2 cups coleslaw mix
- 1 cup unsweetened pineapple tidbits, drained, 3 tablespoons liquid reserved
- 2 green onions, chopped
- 1/2 cup reduced-fat mayonnaise
- 6 hoagie buns, split and toasted
- 4 tablespoons reduced-fat tartar sauce
- 3 medium tomatoes, sliced

Directions:

1. Preheat oven to 400°.
2. Pour egg substitute into a shallow bowl.
3. In a separate shallow bowl, mix bread crumbs and Creole seasoning.
4. Dip shrimp in egg substitute, then in crumb mixture, patting to help coating adhere.
5. Bake in a greased pan until shrimp turn pink, 7-9 minutes. Keep warm.
6. Add crushed pineapple (with juice), and mix well. Do not drain your pineapple!
7. Mix in whipped topping. Stir in bananas, marshmallows, fruit cocktail, and mandarin oranges.
8. Cover, and refrigerate until thoroughly chilled.
9. Combine broccoli slaw, pineapple and green onions. In a small bowl, whisk together mayonnaise and reserved pineapple liquid until smooth. Add to broccoli mixture; toss to coat.
10. To serve, spread hoagie buns with tartar sauce. Divide tomato slices and shrimp among buns. Top with pineapple broccoli slaw.

READERS GUIDE

1. Summer Island is full of passionate residents. Do you live in a community with people who like to debate over issues?

2. Why do you think Trace didn't lean on Kat, Jewels, Wind, and Bri about what had happened in Brazil?

3. How do you think you'd feel after the death of an intern that you were responsible for?

4. Dustin stated he'd moved to Summer Island after being coaxed into it by Trevor, but his friend says he did it to be near Trace. Why do you think Dustin made the move?

5. Have you ever been manipulated by someone like Rhonda manipulated Dustin about tearing down the shack? How did that make you feel? How did you handle the situation?

6. What do you think helped Dustin realize he wasn't too self-absorbed to deserve Trace?

7. Have you ever known a person willing to face his worst fears to help you the way Dustin jumped into

the ocean to save Trace when he thought she was drowning?

8. Did you have sympathy for Rhonda after learning why she was upset that Trace's father didn't leave his home to her? Do you think things would've been different between her and the Summer Island Sisters if Rhonda had grown up without abandonment issues?

9. Would you have been Team Dustin or Team Trace?

10. If you were able to visit Summer Island for a day what would you like to do? Go out sailing on Trevor's boat? Go shopping with Wind? Perhaps hang out on Friendship Beach for cocktails and talking about books.

ALSO BY CIARA KNIGHT

For a complete list of my books, please visit my website at www. ciaraknight.com. A great way to keep up to date on all releases, sales and prizes subscribe to my Newsletter. I'm extremely sociable, so feel free to chat with me on Facebook, Twitter, or Goodreads.

For your convenience please see my complete title list below, in reading order:

CONTEMPORARY ROMANCE

Friendship Beach Series

Summer Island Book Club

Summer Island Sisters

And More

Sweetwater County Series

Winter in Sweetwater County

Spring in Sweetwater County

Summer in Sweetwater County

Fall in Sweetwater County

Christmas in Sweetwater County

Valentines in Sweet-water County

Fourth of July in Sweetwater County

Thanksgiving in Sweetwater County

Grace in Sweetwater County

Faith in Sweetwater County

Love in Sweetwater County

A Sugar Maple Holiday Novel

(Historical)

If You Keep Me

If You Choose Me

A Sugar Maple Novel

If You Love Me

If You Adore Me

If You Cherish Me

If You Hold Me

If You Kiss Me

Riverbend

In All My Wishes

In All My Years

In All My Dreams

In All My Life

A Christmas Spark

A Miracle Mountain Christmas

HISTORICAL WESTERNS:

McKinnie Mail Order Brides Series

Love on the Prairie

ABOUT THE AUTHOR

Ciara Knight is a USA TODAY Bestselling Author, who writes clean and wholesome romance novels set in either modern day small towns or wild historic old west. Born with a huge imagination that usually got her into trouble, Ciara is happy she's found a way to use her powers for good. She loves spending time with her characters and hopes you do, too.

Manufactured by Amazon.ca
Bolton, ON

27902633R00111